Diary of Margery Blake

The following is my own account of my life, as it is. For those reading my pages, I ask only this, that you do not judge me harshly. For am I not the creation of this society that has deemed women inferior? I have fought against such constraints for so long. In my youth, my rebellious behaviour was tolerated. Now aged eighteen, it is no longer voiced and an unspoken truce has been declared. I was never granted leave to voice my own terms of this truce between myself and my parents. It was merely understood and accepted that I, Margery Rose Blake, would endeavor to become the lady expected of me, and achieve a husband worthy of my status. It seems my father has made his choice, and thus my own life has ended, and another chosen for me.

February 1st 1853

I have kept diaries of my childhood, but they were a mere scribbling of a youngster and not of much interest to anyone, including myself, and so they were thrust into a drawer for many years, before finally finding their way to the fire. Now in my eighteenth year, I feel a compulsion to re-visit my old habit and have decided to make notes of my life, for my own interest. Surely there can be a small joy to look back on such writings in many years to come, and see my own history written in my hand. It is my only control within my life after all. Or perhaps my vanity overwhelms my senses, and nothing I write can be of interest? However, as this is the path I have chosen, I shall attempt to convey what is happening in my surroundings. Yet, I am jumping ahead, and that will never do. Though I cannot lie, I feel a small shudder of excitement at moving against what is expected. A tiny victory at best, but a victory nonetheless.

For in my circles, it would be considered rude and dishonourable to move at such a pace, when it is expected that the pace shall be done at the 'proper' measure. Though in truth, I doubt anyone truly knows who decided on such a thing, or why, but there it is. All things must be done accordingly, and so in true Victorian style I shall attempt to write my diary in such a way that you, the reader, will not be offended, and my honour, such as it is, will not be questioned.

My name as is already mentioned is Miss Margery Rose Blake. I have recently been informed that I am expected to marry a man almost twice my age, though he has not asked my father's permission as yet. His proposal is expected at any moment, and it is hoped that I shall marry and be Mrs Margery Rose Harrison by the spring.

My mother confided in me after dinner this evening that Captain John Harrison of the 4th Queen's own Regiment of Light Dragoons would be dining with us tomorrow evening, and it is hoped by both of our parents that he approaches father afterwards.

I confess, my mouth was open. I formed the words of disdain in my head, but they never left my mind. I quickly closed my mouth and turned away to allow Betsy, my maid to help me remove my dress. I barely listened to my mother's excited chatter about weddings and bridal gowns and whom to invite; it meant nothing to me. This would be their wedding, not mine.

I am merely a pawn, nothing more. I am a daughter to marry off into another prominent family which would in turn relieve my father of the burden of paying for my upkeep. It seemed eighteen years was long enough to live under his roof, and if all went to their plan, I would be away on my honeymoon before my nineteenth birthday. Wed and a woman in the true sense.

Perhaps I should say a little regarding my intended. Captain John Harrison or Captain John, as he has always been known to me, does not seem to be a particularly unkind man. He isn't ugly or fat. He is tall, perhaps nearing six feet and is considered quite a catch in our circles. Many a young girl has commented in secret on his fine looks. Not I, for he wears a moustache, which I despise. My opinion goes against the common thoughts on moustaches. To me they look like hairy slugs that hide a man's smile. My parents attended his thirtieth birthday a few months ago but I declined, feigning a headache.

The truth was, I had no intention of taking the limelight on his birthday, when the entire county was expecting a proposal shortly. It seemed improper to have all eyes on me, and 'us' if he'd talked to me. The gossip was hard enough to bear. I refused to endure it during his celebration.

The Harrisons have been family friends for years, though I barely knew them. My father and Sir George had gone to war together, fighting in the same regiment and returning in one piece, before I was born. Whatever they had endured, had made them friends for life, though father rarely spoke of his past adventures abroad' as he called it. John, Sir George's youngest son has followed his father's example and fought in the Afghan war which he called 'The Auckland Folly' for some dreary reason I don't care to know. Having survived with only a few scrapes, he made Captain of his regiment.

His brother Richard, three years older, is something to do with finances though in truth, I care very little. He has been married these last five years to Anne, his second wife. His first died in childbirth eight years before. I don't remember her well. Long dark hair and mournful eyes, but I was a child, running around the gardens, taking little notice of our guests.

Thankfully, we barely see Richard, or his wife, to which I must admit to some relief. Richard makes me feel all the more uncomfortable than Captain John. I'll catch him staring at me with a strange smile on his face. He has no moustache to hide his full lips, mores' the pity. Whenever we have the misfortune to meet at parties or dinners, I find him false, as if he is playing some secret part in a play, and we are his characters, though we have no idea of his folly.

Captain John is always courteous to me but he is nothing to me. I feel little, if anything towards him when he calls. I feel nothing when he leaves. I exchange conversation with him, but never on any intimate terms, and never alone. He remains a gentleman throughout and has never expressed his affection to me; of that I am glad. Still, my heart remains beating the same and I experience no fluttering in my stomach or lady parts – (I check that my door is firmly closed after I write such lewd words) but it is true.

My older sister Katherine, married three years and already carrying her second child, confided in me when Sir David Edgeworthy courted her that she'd felt a strange sensation in her unspeakable and wondered what it meant. After her wedding, we'd spoken briefly on the subject whilst giggling into our cups of tea one sunny afternoon.

"I believe it's my womanhood telling me that I'm in love and David is the right man for me."

I blushed, a deep red, and hid my face behind my cup but still felt a strong urge to hear more on such a forbidden subject.

"Do you still feel this sensation ... down there ...?" I'd asked meekly.

Katherine, all grown up and married less than a month had merely smiled, nodded and clamped her mouth firmly shut, as David walked in from his shooting party.

I felt none of this for Captain John. Nothing in my body reacted, even on the few occasions he'd kissed my hand, nothing. It was like he didn't exist, but a mere shadow to be indulged during our frequent dinners and occasional parties. He never invaded my dreams, or my thoughts whilst awake.

Whilst growing up, we barely moved in the same circles. He is twelve years older, and was not interested in a young girl. Besides, his family frequently move in slightly higher circles than our family, and I have often pondered why Sir George and Gloria bother with us at all; beyond my father's connection, we have very little in common.

My father worked in finance after he returned home from the war and made a fair amount, judging from our standard of living. We have a large home on the outskirts of Horsham with a small staff. My father would travel into London regularly and stay at his club. Here, he frequently met with Sir George, and this is possibly where he approached the subject of a match.

Ever since my parents broached the possibility of a marriage proposal I admit, he has entered my head, but as a conundrum. He's shown no obvious affection towards me, and yet my parents who know more about it than I, are convinced of his intentions.

I can see nothing in my appearance that would ignite his affection. I am a graceful dancer, if I may permit a small indulgence, and many a man has fought for my card, which is full at every ball. I am neither good looking, nor plain. My bosom is small, as is my waist, but it could be better and I work with Betsy every morning to pull my corset tight. My brown hair has a slight wave in it, but is thin, and the ends break easily, but once it is styled, it looks like everyone else's. However, once loose, and down my back, it looks like a mad fox's tail!

I look up into the large oval mirror that is attached to my dressing table. My hazel eyes look back at me. They are not ugly eyes, but wide and bright and my lashes seem longer than Katherine's. I press my nose this way and that; small and petite. Thankfully I did not inherit my father's large nose. I purse my lips and blow myself a kiss. My top lip is fuller than my bottom, but neither has felt a man's touch, especially one with a hairy slug on top of it!

I slowly trace my neck down to my collar bone which is a little protruding, but no more so than other girls my age.

My fingers travel down to the top of my small breasts and I shiver with the sensation. If I marry Captain John, I will become his, meaning he will own me and everything on me, and anything owned can be touched. I suddenly feel something for Captain John. Revulsion.

February 2nd 1853

Last night's revelation disturbed me enough to keep me awake for the majority of the dark hours. I fell into an exhausted slumber sometime around dawn as the birds began to wake. Betsy was punctual as always and brought my cup of tea a couple of hours later with her usual smile.

She talked of another lovely day intermingled with a tiny bit of gossip regarding one of the gardeners and a local girl from the village.

All of which I ignore as best as I can as I force my eyes to open and push my sensitive body upwards into a seated position to accept my tea.

Betsy stopped her incessant chatter and finally looked at me. I must have looked awful as she quickly came to feel my brow and fret over me until I batted her away like an annoying fly. I cannot recall what I said to her, but it was rude enough to stop her from fussing and she went instead to gather my clothes for the day. I feel remorse and debate calling her to apologise, but etiquette stops me and I firmly shut my mouth. My head aches and my eyes feel sore. I yearn to return to any slumber that was available but if I do not show to breakfast, my mother will venture upstairs to question my absence and it would become more trouble than it is worth.

Forcing the lukewarm tea down my dry throat I allow Betsy to help me wash and dress. The only part I enjoy is when she does my hair. Her fingers are so light and quick, it feels delightful on my scalp and as she brushes with long strokes, my head tingles, and I feel the tension in my shoulders reduce.

I smile kindly and thank her, hoping that is enough of an apology for my earlier mood. Although Betsy smiles back, I am never sure what she thinks or feels and although my mother pounded into Katherine and me that relationships with the staff must be kept at arm's length and proper, I can't help but wish sometimes that Betsy could be more than my maid.

Perhaps I should write a small description of Betsy to help you 'see' her in your mind's eye. I believe that she is four years older than myself and has brothers, one of which works in the stables, as does an older cousin. Betsy Wainwright has been with us since she was about thirteen, working her way up the kitchens from scullery to parlour maid until the housekeeper, Mrs. Elsa Williams, considered her hard-working enough to be trained up as a house maid, and eventually, a ladies' maid. As the youngest daughter, it seemed that I was lumbered with her as she moved upstairs. As it happened, we got on, at least as well as one can with a maid.

When my courses began five years ago, Betsy was the one who explained what they were and why they happened. She then went to tell Elsa, to explain the dirty laundry who then informed my mother, who hurried upstairs and planted a kiss on my forehead as I lay in bed feeling dirty and shocked by this new turn of events.

The following day, Betsy had been allocated to me as my own ladies' maid and that gained her an extra two pounds. I only know this as I'd had the audacity to ask her one evening how much a ladies' maid earned and was shocked to hear the mere amount of twenty pounds a year. I consider this to be a terrible fault of my father, but Betsy assures me that she is happy, considering she gets a bed and is fed three meals a day.

Since that night we have been on fairly good terms. Betsy tells me everything that happens below stairs, and any gossip she hears from the village, whilst I share occasional discreet gossip that I hear during parties that I consider in good taste, and nothing that would demean the name of those involved.

Besides, the servants hear of it sooner or later. I've become aware through Betsy that the servant's gossip line is far and wide and downstairs is usually a party of conversation regarding someone or other. Yet I digress. This morning I know is going to be a difficult morning to get through. I am on edge, exhausted and my courses are due, which always leaves me feeling out of sorts with anyone whom I perceive as an annoyance. Spending the day with my mother was not going to go well.

Betsy had just finished doing my hair when Mother came in beaming. Dismissing Betsy, she takes both of my hands and tells me the news I dread. Captain John Harrison has sent word that he is coming for morning tea, and has asked to speak with Father beforehand. It seems that evening dinner is too long for him to wait.

Mother's excitement is overwhelming, and I let her babble on about how wonderful it will be and what a beautiful bride I'll make, with a man from the regiment. In her excitement she doesn't notice my hands become hot and sweaty. Mother doesn't see that I merely stare at her and show no enthusiasm whatsoever. She notices nothing, other than the great possibility that both her daughters will be married, to well established families, and that she has done her job as our mother.

I should point out at this time that growing up, Katherine and I barely saw our mother. Our nurse brought us up and then a governess took over for a while until she left under strange circumstances last year, but as I was nearing eighteen, they decided not to advertise for another. Besides, it was expected that I would marry and the search began for a proper suitor. Captain John Harrison had apparently shown an interest and the game began, at least, I'm told it did, but I was not a player, merely a pawn in my family's chess game.

I flee to the large gardens once I'd endured breakfast, of which I barely ate. Mother put it down to nerves and she is correct in her assumption, but not correct in why. It is accepted that I shall not refuse Captain John; why would I? He is expected to go far within the regiment. He has shown great valour in the Afghan war, and has saved many of his men, giving orders that showed a good head for battle strategies. He has received a slash to his torso, or so I understand.

He comes from a prominent family of the county who have connections to royalty, and he is considered the best option for a second daughter. If I refuse him, it is doubtful I will have many options left. I would dishonour my family by becoming an old maid, a burden or worse, a governess. The options were preferable to me whilst they caused my mother to have fainting fits when she considered them.

I pace the immaculate lawn, aware that eyes follow my route, and whispers behind the glass windows, though unheard by my ears, were shouting loudly in my head. "Where is she going? Keep an eye on her whereabouts so that we may inform Captain John when he arrives. A proposal in the garden on such a glorious day is so romantic."

I hide from prying eyes behind a cluster of thick rhododendrons, and catch my breath, as my corset only allows short breaths. I glance around me like a caged animal, and find myself moving towards the narrow, hedge-lined lane that runs beside our home. I know of course, that it leads towards the village, over a mile away, but it also has plenty of tracks and footpaths that allow someone to wander over fields and woodland. To escape these confines is my only thought.

I am halfway to the village before I stop at an open field, and gaze out at the countryside I have grown to love. It is fairly warm for February, though a chill still hangs in the air, and I wrap my arms around me for warmth.

I stare out at the fields that I can see for miles. I probably won't see them blossom into gold, and yellows, and greens, in the summer. I touch the hedge nearest to me and look down at the soil beneath it. I'd not see the wild flowers that would spring up along the lane. I will miss everything familiar to me if I marry that stranger.

At this moment I feel empty. No need to put on airs and graces for visitors. No need to pretend I am interested in conversations that bore me to tears. No need to be swept away by what everyone else considers best for me. I am alone. I am myself and I know that I cannot marry Captain John Harrison and be happy.

I have no concept of how long I stood staring out at the vastness of nature, but a polite cough interrupted my gaze and I turn towards the sound. I recognise him immediately; it is one of our gardeners, though his name is a mystery. On seeing he has my attention, he abruptly pulls off his cap and holds it tightly in his big hands.

He looks nervous, but stands up straight to inform me that my family is looking for me. He continues to tell me that he'd spied my leaving, and had undertaken the job of bringing me back safely without divulging my whereabouts to my parents.

There was a long silence between us as I fight my instincts to run, but the truth is, I have nowhere to run to. He knows it as much as I, and after a long time, he cautiously steps closer and surveys the land before us.

"Beautiful isn't it my lady ... my grandfather ploughed this land. He had a farm just over that hill there."

I turn to where he points. I can smell his sweat which isn't unduly unpleasant, but stirs in me something I don't recognise.

"It is beautiful. I love the way the sky touches the hills over there. Everything here is free to do whatever it needs to do."

I blush then embarrassed that I have spoken so freely with this employee of my father's, and move away from him, stepping back into the lane.

Together we walk home, though on nearing my father's house, he abruptly replaces his cap, bids me a good day, and leaves me there, while he walks swiftly in another direction before being seen. I silently thank him, take a long deep breath, and enter the garden, where I escaped hours before to await my fate. Captain John is the first to spy me, as I venture out from behind the bushes. He is sitting with my mother in the conservatory, while my father paces the garden, shouting orders to various staff that they find me immediately. It does not pass my attention that Captain John does not stand immediately, but watches my approach with a look in his eyes that I cannot read, but only aids in making me feel even more uncomfortable. Finally my mother sees me, and her cries of delight catch Father's attention, and only then does Captain John stand as is required in polite society, and a smile breaks the tension in his face.

I remember wondering if I have been mistaken in my opinion of him, as he makes a fuss about my reappearance and asks me if my walk has been refreshing. I answer politely that it has, but I was in need of refreshment due to the chill of the morning. I am aware all the time that my parents are fighting the urge to scold me, whilst knowing that it would not be courteous to do so in front of my intended.

I take the opportunity to refresh myself with tea, refusing a scone, and wait behind my cup for the inevitable. It isn't long before my parents excuse themselves, and finally I am left alone with my future. Captain John says nothing untoward, but sips his own tea whilst staring ahead at the nearby willow tree. The silence becomes unbearable, and I shift in my seat. The blanket wrapped around my legs becoming itchy. If this is his punishment for me running off this morning, he can sit here himself. I put down my empty cup and stand. He immediately does the same.

"Shall we stroll awhile or have you had enough of walking?"

I can read nothing on his face, but my
instincts tell me that he is not pleased
with my obvious escape, and my stomach
constricts with trepidation as we wander
slowly, and silently, among the flower
beds, in full view of the house. It is during
the second turn of the garden that he
stops, turns and steps in front of me,
causing me to halt and step backwards.
Taking my hand he smiles, though no
warmth ensues from it, and he says the
words I dread.

"Be my wife." It isn't a question, it is an
order. No bended knee, no love, no
sincerity, but an order he expects to be
obeyed. I desperately want to refuse him,
but my breeding and my parent's
expectations over-ride this instinct, and I
merely nod in compliance.

"Say yes." His command needs more than
a nod. Captain John demands the word to
humiliate me further, knowing I hold no
love for him, but he will own me
regardless.

"Yes." There, I say it.

Captain John kisses the hand he holds before releasing it quickly, and we walk towards the house, where I can see my parents at the window, already ordering for the champagne that is chilling in the kitchens. I feel nothing. I toast myself, and accept the congratulations. I smile when expected, and listen as Mother talks of colours and organising and bridal gowns, but not once do I look at my future husband, until he departs, and only then do I watch him mount his horse and ride away, and wish he'll never return.

I confess I feel evil in my thoughts and pray God will bring about some natural disaster that would ensure Captain John Harrison never returns to my home. I can suffer the humiliation of being abandoned, though I doubt my parents could. They would consider it a most dishonourable act. However, I find this scenario more acceptable than the fast approaching wedding, and its night.

February 7th 1853

It has been five days since the proposal, and the days are a blur of material, invitations, flowers and ribbons. I am having to choose bridesmaids from among my cousins, and of course, Katherine is my matron of honour. She, along with my mother, is a constant companion these last few days. Along with aunts and cousins, who all want to impart their knowledge onto me.
I confess that I hear none of it and cannot recite any of their wisdom. I merely show up every day, and allow my mother and Katherine to do whatever they choose to do. I stand where they tell me, lift my arms when told and nod in all the right places, as they enthuse over the design of my wedding gown.
I barely eat. Sleep is minimal as I toss and turn with terrible nightmares. In the last week I have endured the poking and prodding of excitable women, along with gut wrenching agonies of womanhood.

That has thankfully passed and I enjoy a long, hot bath in our new copper bathtub, and refuse to feel guilt, as the maids carry the hot water. I have no peace, and I worry that I shall never have it again.

February 15th 1853

My life flees so quickly, I have not written. Perhaps it is due to the fact that I have had nothing to write except 'God help me' these last few days, as everything is finalised and nothing untoward has happened to my betrothed. He appears regularly for dinner and today he met us for afternoon tea in town. We barely speak. I allowed my mother to fill in any awkward silences and I answer his rare questions with short sentences, and very little eye contact.

Captain John behaves impeccably throughout and wins the admiration of my mother, as she chastises me for my curt responses following our tea.

I attempt to care, to feel something, but all I can muster is the horror of having to be alone with this stranger.

Following our tea, we visit a few shops to purchase ribbon and some thread for the bridesmaid's dresses, that are to be a rose pink. My gown is well underway of ivory and white, to represent my innocence. I dwell on this as we make our home in the carriage. Thankfully, Mother allows me time in silence, as she contemplates her many tasks in getting me wed.

My innocence in all things of man. That is what my dress is representing and until that night, it will be a true reflection of me, yet by nightfall, I shall be spoilt and humiliated, purely so that my husband can lay claim to me. Betsy attempts to ask me about my knowledge of men, but we are interrupted by one of my cousins, and the matter is dropped. I shall endeavour to bring about the conversation again as I feel sure that the more information I have, the less terrible it will seem.

February 21st 1853

I am undone! I am in despair! Betsy has just left me. Finally, I managed to bring the conversation around to the wedding night and men, much to my shame and trepidation. I get the words out of my mouth before I can change my mind. Betsy had been undoing my hair, carefully finding the pins and letting the hair uncurl and fall to my waist. I believe that she could see, if not feel my anxiety as I am fidgeting, while I attempt to muster the words to convey my horror. Finally, they come out, and Betsy stops what she was doing and stares at my reflection in the mirror.

"Your mother has not spoken of this to you, Miss?"

I shake my head and look away, my face a burning crimson. I feel such shame. I must admit to still feeling nausea even now. An hour or more has passed since Betsy informed me of what was to pass between me and Captain John. I gaze down at my nightgown to the place where my legs connect to my hips, and slowly reach out to touch myself there.

"It will hurt, at least the first time, but after that, I am told it is pleasurable," Betsy said, and smiled.

What else could she tell me? Her own lack of experience limited her knowledge, but her mother had thankfully passed on the facts, and now I knew of them also.

How can a man fit? As a child, I watched fascinated as my sister used the chamber pot, and knowing my own experiences, I could not see how a man could put his 'thing' into such a small hole that allowed water to leave my body.

I asked Betsy this, but she merely shrugged, and said that there was a way in, and this was also the place babies came out. I gaze down for a long time, willing myself to find the courage to look, but I do not, and eventually, I crawl into bed and attempt to sleep.

February 25th 1853

It is evening and Captain John and his ghastly parents have finally left us, following an evening of bridge and dinner. I retire almost as soon as they leave, not through exhaustion as I proclaim, but a need to be alone and fight down the nerves that flutter endlessly in my stomach. Gloria, Captain John's mother, commented on my thinness and hopes I won't fade away to nothing before I wear my wedding gown. I merely stare back at her, and thankfully, Mother took over the conversation about what is expected of girls and dresses, and Gloria ignores me for the rest of the evening.

I remove my dress before Betsy arrives, and stare at my reflection. Gloria is right, I have become so thin, my bones protrude; I look ghastly. So long have I fought with Betsy to fit into my corset, always hoping for a thinner waist. Now, I have one, and skeletal arms and legs to match. Will my husband want this new body? To starve myself to death seems more preferable to allowing a stranger to put his 'thing' into me, and hurt me.

Betsy arrives and helps me out of my corset and into my nightgown. She says very little, but I see the looks she gives me and I know I have at least one ally. The wedding is set for the 15th of April. According to my mother, I shall be the perfect spring bride as the cherry blossoms around the churchyard sprinkle me with their buds.

I sit now in my large bed, and ponder how it will feel, to be lying with another human being, under covers, and our bodies close and touching? I have shared a bed with my sister on many occasions as children, but never as women. Will Captain John be hairy and sweaty? Will his body stink? I recall the smell of sweat on the gardener's body and found that smell not un-pleasant. Or had it been the man that I'd found pleasing, and his smell was irrelevant?

I cannot deny that the gardener is pleasing on the eyes, and his smile is acceptable, as are his dark, blue eyes and his rather large hands. I compare his form to that of Captain John, and find the latter most wanting.

February 28th 1853

I endure yet another visit from Captain John and his mother, thankfully, his father is engaged elsewhere. Out of all three, Sir George is the most bearable, mainly due to the fact he barely speaks to me, preferring my father's company. We stroll in the park opposite my parent's home as the spring is slowly descending onto the earth. It truly is glorious watching the many colours begin to protrude upwards.

Daffodil and crocus peep out from everywhere and buds are forming on all the surrounding trees. Children play around us, while couples share a blanket here and there on the few benches littered around the walkways, whilst others stroll arm in arm. I walk separately from Captain John, while our mothers follow behind. I can almost feel my mother's eyes burning into my back, as I behave as though he were not even here.

He spoke on occasion about various people we saw, and the heat of the sun, but beyond that, we walk in silence.

When our mothers catch up, we stop for tea at a quaint tearoom. Captain John enquires about the wedding gown and the preparations, which in turn, give our mothers, leave to discuss invitations, and those they have received. I catch his eye as they converse in earnest and see something in his face that makes me stare all the more. He is enjoying himself, knowing that I am not. He knows of my loathing for this union, and he has brought up the wedding conversation, knowing it will make me uncomfortable – and that brings him pleasure.

Even now, as I write these words, I am fearful of this man. A man who only months ago I had considered no threat to me. It may be my imagination. It may be that I am searching for any excuse to hate him, and yet I cannot get that look on his face out of my thoughts.

March 3rd 1853

I am ill. I have taken to my bed since yesterday afternoon with a fever. I have finally been left alone to rest following the physician's visit and he bled me, which I find intolerable, but felt too weak to argue. Besides, I am merely a woman, a weaker sex in a man's eye and therefore, who would take any notice of my cares? Doctor Hobson certainly would not. He would declare that he brought me into this world, and saw to my every health concerns since and will continue to do so until either one of us dies. I had hoped it would be me last night, but I am still here.

Flowers arrived this morning from Captain John. Betsy put them on my dresser, I have put them in my wardrobe; I have no wish to see them and be reminded of who sent them. It may be that I am delirious and am not thinking correctly, but when I look at his 'gift', all I see is a lie.

I feel that he has bought the flowers out of duty, not love or care and so I refuse to indulge and move them. No doubt, Mother will question the whereabouts of his offering, and I will use such a question to bring up my own - why must I marry? I have pondered this question over and over and I am sure that it is this anxiety that has made me thus. I am so fraught with this burden of marriage to Captain John, I can barely endure a day; I feel so overwhelmed with fear.

I am determined to broach the subject of marrying this man with my mother, whom I hope will reassure me that I do not have to go through with it. Surely a parent's love is stronger, and more worthy, than pawning off their daughter? I cannot reconcile myself to such a barbarous action, and am convinced that I would never allow it with my own.

March 7th 1853

I have not had the heart to write. My body, racked with fever is weakened but I am assured that I am mending. Rest and fresh air will be my medicine; or so my mother is guaranteed by Doctor Hobson. I know that my only medicine is to withdraw from this engagement, and move far away from the prying eyes of family.

I finally spoke with Mother last night. I have been in and out of sleep, and could barely speak as my throat constricted in dryness and sharp pains. Last night, following a small amount of honey and brandy, I felt able to voice my horror at such a union.

At first, I was not sure that she had heard me, and I began in earnest to convey my fear at marrying such a man. On which she abruptly turned and glared at me with such anger that I have not seen before. She called me 'ungrateful', 'spoilt', amongst other names that have me shocked to my very soul.

"It is an honour to be asked by such a man and from a prominent family; you couldn't do better."

I tried to convey how much I don't care
for him but she cut me off.

"You will marry him and bring forth sons
and soon you will deem this conversation
folly. You may not love him, but you will
learn. Not all relationships can be for
love; that is a romantic notion. I will not
hear another word on this."

And she left me.

I remain staring at the closed door for a
long time, willing her to return and
comfort me, but she does not. It is now
nearing dinner, and still Mother does not
return to check on my wellbeing. Betsy is
hovering throughout the day, but she
says very little and keeps her gaze
downwards. I believe the whole household
now knows of my plight, and no one will
save me.

March 12th 1853

I am much better, in that my fever has gone, and my courses have come with a vengeance, whilst I was recovering. I use this as a further excuse to remain in my bed for longer. I have been informed that Captain John is enquiring on my health, to be told that I am recovering perfectly. 'Perfectly'? I am a woman who is being offered to him, there is nothing 'perfect' about that, and yet I can do nothing about it.

Betsy confided yesterday that my father is outraged at my conversation with Mother regarding this marriage, and would have me wed the moment I am feeling better if it were not for the preparations already made. She also told me that my wedding gown is finished and is hanging in Mother's room - I care for none of it and say as much.

Betsy bade me to be careful in voicing my opinions so freely and loudly, and I thank her for her care. Today I am up and about, sitting in my favourite place, the window seat of my bedroom with the window slightly ajar, to allow air into my lungs.

I feel as weak as a kitten following the fever, and the heavy bleeding. I now have time again to consider my future - such as it is.

One month until I am wed. One month to get to full strength and gain weight as I look skeletal and pale, which is inconceivable for a happy, blushing bride - apparently. According to Betsy, my mother has ordered that my food portions should be doubled, and that I should consume more milk, and meat, to gain strength. The household have a month to make me look pleasing to the eye of my impending husband. Betsy told me in confidence that the servants, especially Elsa, the cook, were under no illusions of what was expected of them, but that they were very much on my side, and consider the union between myself and Captain John a bad one.

March 19th 1853

I sit outside in our garden for most of the morning. I even take a short stroll around the borders, as Katherine comes to visit and help with the preparations. Mother has summoned her, to help with changing my sullen face, into a happier one – she has failed.

Katherine also wants to be present when Mother forces me to try on the wedding gown. Much to their horror, I have lost so much weight, it hangs on me. I stand still, while the seamstress makes adjustments. I stand still while they prattle around me, pulling the fabric this way and that, making comments, shaking their heads – I stare straight ahead at the clouds passing the window.

Following luncheon, Katherine and I are left alone. I have no doubt that this was on Mother's terms, as before she had even disappeared inside the house, Katherine was leaning forward, a look of concern on her face.

"Are you so nervous dearest?" she asked me.

I will admit to being so close to giving way to my emotions that I almost blurt out everything, but hold it back. For I know that everything I speak of will go back to Mother, and no doubt, Father, and I can see no point in continuing this torturous journey. My destination is set. I have no control and everyone knows it. I merely nod and let Katherine make up her own mind of the nature of my nervousness. Of course, she chooses the wedding night, which is only one of the many worries that I have and I allow her to think it.

She repeats to me what I have already heard from Betsy. That it will hurt, at least for the first time, and there will be bleeding, but I was not to fret about that. Bleeding is a good sign. I consider asking how bleeding can possibly be construed as a 'good sign', but hold my tongue and merely nod and attempt a thin smile, in the hope of putting her obvious awkwardness to rest - it worked. We sat in compatible silence for a while, before the crying of her child sent her in that direction of the house.

I watch my sister leave with a heavy heart. We were once so close, sharing every secret and information gleamed from our childhood. Yet now, she is a stranger to me. She is a woman with Katherine's face, yet, she is no longer a sister, but a mother and wife of which I have no claim. I am the younger sister who needs to wed, and gain my own family, in her eyes. Katherine is embracing motherhood, and wifely duties, with a passion I cannot contemplate. She loves her husband David; I despise my intended.

March 22nd 1853

Captain John visits me this afternoon. He brought with him a gift of a brush and mirror. Both are decorated with fine embroidery on the back and are indeed, beautiful. I accept them with a slight smile, and thank him for his gift. My mother was so much more enthusiastic than I, and it was not lost on anyone within the room.

I am fully recovered of my illness, and have since found that there have been many who succumbed to this influenza that swept through Sussex County, killing a handful of the elderly and the very young. Most deaths occurred in the poorer area, where the penniless and hungry reside.

I admit to feeling melancholy on the subject of those lives lost, and consider that saving my wretched body was a tragedy. I caught this illness due to my melancholia of my circumstance, I am certain of it. I am sure that God knows what he is doing and that his plans are worthy of me.

Captain John informs us that almost half of his father's household has been afflicted, though all have recovered sufficiently to return to work. I ask him if he has endured any illness. He has not. "I have never been ill Madam. I have a healthy constitution and expect to continue in such a vein. God willing of course."

Mother immediately congratulates him on such health whilst giving me a look of reproach, for I have not attempted to disguise my wish that he be ill – and Captain John knows it. I am chastised the moment we are out of his ear shot. I don't care and say as much. Mother merely glares at me and walks away. I am left shaking with my boldness and say as much to Betsy later.

"You'd best be careful Miss, or else you may jeopardise this engagement with your conduct. No man wants to marry a woman with such opinions and attitudes. You are making it too obvious of your hatred of him. It will not be in your favour to gain his anger before you are even wed."

I know that Betsy is correct, and yet I cannot help myself. My horror at having to share my life with this man grows with each passing day and the nights are spent in turmoil at having his hands on me.

My mind tries desperately to find a
happy memory, and strangely, always
the gardener appears in my mind. Now
there is a man I believe I could love, if I
were indeed free to choose as commoners
are. Oh, how I am jealous of their freedom
to love.

March 25th 1853

Oh God! It is merely two weeks until the
end of my life. Preparations are done. I
admit, the dresses are beautiful despite
my terror. I cannot deny that they are
exquisite and if it were anything but my
wedding I would be happy to wear any of
them. They are now hanging in one of the
unoccupied bedrooms.
The flowers are arranged and the church
is waiting our arrival. The bands have
been read for all to hear and I felt myself
die just a little on hearing them said out
loud.

The vicar of our local parish is a quiet, kind man, whom I have spoken to on occasions regarding the scriptures and stories within the Bible. I have considered confessing to him my fears, but so far, I remain silent. When he asks if there is any reason for us not to wed, I am sure to bite down on my lip so as not to scream out 'yes'.

Captain John's visits are becoming more frequent, and I cannot fathom why. I deduce that it must be to check that his bride-to-be has not fled, or that my health has not conveniently faltered. I pray daily that the fever returns, and the wedding is cancelled. Of course, I know this to be folly, as it would only be postponed. Better to get it over with now perhaps?

We walk around the garden which is flourishing with colour and scent. Of the gardener, I never see him. I tell no one of my thoughts of him, but perhaps good looking young men are kept away from young brides, just in case?

We walk in the park and around town, and dine almost every night, with various friends and family. We never sit together, and we very rarely speak, except in polite conversation. Captain John talks mainly with Father and any other men in the party. It is usually about various battles, war, hunting, fishing and the government - all of which bore me. I know nothing of war and fighting. I despise hunting, and politics has never been explained to me, so I know nothing on the subject.

I catch him watching me on occasion and feel my cheeks blush a bright red. He smiles on seeing my discomfort and I hate him for it. I stare at his moustache when I think he isn't looking and recoil at such an ugly thing. He kisses my hand when we meet, and when he leaves, and that is enough to make my stomach knot in revulsion. I can feel it on my skin and know that in a couple of weeks, that moustache will be on my face. I feel sick.

April 2nd 1853

I made myself ill again through lack of eating. My stomach is in such a constant knot of terror that eating only causes more pain, and I either vomit, which is most uncomfortable and disgusting, or I nibble on small things and hope they remain inside me. I have lost more weight and look pale and ill. Mother is beside herself with the wedding so close. Not that I gained much weight since my fever, but whatever I had, has now gone and I hear Betsy's intake of breath when she sees me undressed. The corset sits loosely on my waist. I can breathe and that is pleasant, but it digs into my hip bone and ribs, which is uncomfortable. I have taken to remaining in my room in my nightgown.

I hear Father this morning, shouting downstairs which was abruptly followed by the appearance of Mother who took one look at me and bellowed for Betsy, who hurries in from the hallway. I presume that she had been loitering as her appearance was so quick. She is ordered to dress me instantly as Captain John has arrived for luncheon.

"I don't care Mother, I am not hungry." I boldly told her, only to be glared at as if I were something she had trodden on. I feel myself flinch under her stare. I have never endured such blatant hatred towards me before, and I am not comfortable with it. I feel a constriction within my throat, and my body shakes with fear.

"You will eat and you will care my girl. You have attempted all manner of ways to reduce John's affections towards you, and abandon this union. Hear me well. It will take place next Friday, and you will encourage his affection, and be a proper wife, or else you will leave this house and never return."

As I write her words, tears fall on the page and I quickly blot them. I have never known true affection from my mother, but to have such loathing bestowed upon me from her is torture to my heart and soul. All the more hurtful, is knowing that they have no care of my own feelings, only that I am theirs to marry to whomever they choose, and if I do not comply - then I am lost to my family.

As for Captain John's apparent 'affection', I know he has none, but say nothing. I dress obediently and go down to eat with my intended. I pass the next few hours in forced conversations, and required consumption, knowing that it will not remain in my stomach for long. I have vomited twice since.

April 14th 1853

I have not written. I did not have the heart to write what is in my mind and soul. Today is my last day of freedom and with it being so pleasant out, I ask permission to walk in the park. It is granted, so long as Katherine accompanies me.
She arrived last night with her brood, and we dined with my intended, his family and close friends. I do not have any close friends of my own to confide in. I was always a fairly shy girl growing up, and so Katherine and I kept each other company.

I did not want to learn the piano, or learn to draw. I was fairly good with needlework, but very slow, much to Mother's annoyance. I found that I could sing, and much to my horror, last night Katherine urged the others in our party to make me sing; I flatly refused.

That is until Captain John came to me and went down on one knee in front of everyone, and begged me to sing to him. There was no love in his face or his actions. He did it purely for his own amusement as he could see how much it affected me to sing in front of such a party. To my everlasting shame, I sang. I was not asked to sing another, and the applause was pitiful and rightly so. My voice was cracked and out of tune.

As Katherine and I walk in the park, I speak of last night and my feelings on it. Katherine answers noncommittal and moves onto other subjects - safe subjects so that there is no tension between us. I am determined to enjoy my last day as a free, unmarried woman and I encourage it.

We speak of various things, such as her child and the one growing in her. We chat about her daily life, gossip about people we both know and for a while, it feels as it did before she wed. I feel the closeness, and know Katherine does too. We watch the ducks on the lake, and the birds in the sky. We marvel at the colour that ignites the park, and enjoy tea at the park's tea room. I didn't want to go home, but as it was getting late, I agreed, besides, Katherine was pining for her daughter.

Would I ever pine for mine? For his? The thought of having his children was abhorrent, but more so, the act of which to get said children, and that would be happening to me tomorrow evening.

On arriving home, we are bombarded by aunts, cousins and uncles, who have travelled for the wedding. For the rest of the day I am never left alone, as one or more family members want to talk with me. By the time we dine with eleven other people of our family, I want nothing more than to curl up in my bed and be alone, but that is not permitted, not yet.

Barely touching my food as nerves flood my trembling body, I am finally allowed to retire for a good night's sleep. Hours have passed since I left them to wallow in my fear of what is to be my fate, and still, sleep has not found me. Although I am not knowledgeable on what will occur on my wedding night, besides a few possible outcomes given to me by Betsy and Katherine, my mind conjures many variations of torture and pain and it is these that are hindering any sleep. May God be with me tomorrow.

April 15th 1853

It is my wedding day. I write this very early in the morning, I have barely touched sleep. I hear the birds awakening and singing, and for once, I despise them their joy. The sky is clear; it will be a glorious day. The sun shall shine down on my day of horror, and I know that I shall yearn to run and be free out on the meadow. There, this shall be my happy thought. Whilst everyone else is joyous on this day I shall be elsewhere, in my meadow.

My wedding day. The day I marry a man I feel nothing but revulsion and loathing for. Whose property I shall become, and a man I suspect has some hatred of me. I admit, I am unsure of this, as I have no experience in love, and yet, my heart tells me that I would know if I was loved. I feel a sense of love from my parents, regardless of their actions towards me. I feel the sisterly love between Katherine and myself, but of Captain John, I feel only fear.

It is an inner instinctual feeling that he is dangerous, and has no regard for me. I never felt it before that day he proposed to me, and have questioned whether it is true, or if it is my mind playing tricks, merely because I do not want to marry him. To make him a monster would justify those feelings. Yet, I cannot forget his behaviour when I returned to the garden and the look in his eye. In fact, his whole 'proposal' was wrong and improper, but that didn't matter to him. No, I am sure there is something wrong, regardless of my trepidation of marriage.

Alas, I can tell no one. Betsy knows of my fear; though no words have passed between us on the subject, I catch her watching me on occasions before looking away. She spies my unhappiness but what can she do? She cannot save me from my fate. She cannot be there to hold my hand tonight.

My wedding night. Katherine has attempted to tell me in a little more detail, what to expect. She has informed me of the pain and the bleeding that will occur, and how it will feel, but having never seen a man naked, her information only makes me even more fearful and restless. I have never kissed a man, beyond my father on his cheek, and men kiss my hand, but my lips have never been touched by a man's mouth.

I look down at myself. I can see my nipples through my night gown. Today, Captain John will see these if he so chooses, and put his 'thing' between my legs somehow. It will hurt, but I am supposed to accept it. I start the day as a 'Miss', and tonight I shall continue as a 'Mrs'.

I am alone but I have no notion of how long I will be. I am aware of noises coming from somewhere within the house. Most likely the scullery maid getting the morning fires lit as there is still a chill in the air. It is barely six in the morning. I sit with my knees drawn up and write this entry on my window seat, as I gaze out at the growing sunrise.

I am determined to enjoy this moment of peace before the storm. This last moment that is my own.

I am left alone again following an early morning cup of tea from Betsy. She smiles at me and reassures me that she will never leave me, but we both know that she is only allowed to live with me, so long as my new husband does not object to her.

She came in quietly, looking towards the bed, and for a second, I saw her face register fear that perhaps I had fled in the night, but then she saw me curled up on the window seat, and she let out a long sigh, and offered me the cup. I took it gratefully and she left me there, informing me that Mother was awake, and taking breakfast in her room. I have perhaps half an hour before I will be expected to embrace the day.

I can write some more, now that I am left alone again. I stand un-moving in the middle of my bedroom, mine for the last time. I force back the tears that threaten to ruin my face as I am dressed, then admired by various people in my family. My mother cried the tears I desperately wanted to shed, but on seeing her weeping, it made my resolution to be dry-eyed even stronger.

Katherine was quiet, studying me on occasion with a slight frown on her face, but heavy with child, she didn't linger for too long and retired to a cooler room until the service. Betsy lingered in the room, helping with my hair, placing white flowers in amongst the entwined curls – I look pretty, if you look beyond the black eyes and pale complexion. I've been given various foods to try, but my stomach refuses all but the dry biscuits I nibble one while Betsy finishes my hair.

I led the way downstairs where Father was waiting impatiently, but on seeing me, he smiled lovingly, and I felt my resolve to remain dry eyed waning. I blinked back the tears and almost fell into his arms, to beg him to release me from this, but he turned away, and barked an order to one of the footmen, and the moment was gone.

The church is but a short ride in the carriage. I allow my father to take my hand and help me step up into the coach. The sun is shining, and so the top had been removed. I cannot hide my face from anyone as we pass a sea of friendly, cheering faces. The staff comes out to wave us off and a few people wave, and cheer to us in the street. I force a smile that seems to encourage them further. I know my father talked about this and that, but I have no recollection on what subject. No doubt, nothing of great importance. Perhaps he felt a need to speak to hide his own apprehension at losing his last daughter. At least, that is what I like to believe and shall not waver from that.

We enter the full church and the service was conducted. Captain John was surrounded by his fellow officers in full uniform. That is all I can truly recall of it. A carpet of red runs down the centre of the aisle, with men on both sides wearing navy blue, with yellow stripes, and scarlet cuffs and collar. All wore their swords, but they had removed their hats. Moustaches were everywhere, and I despised every last one of them, especially the man standing next to me, speaking clearly his vows; we'd barely looked at each other. The vows done, we walk out as husband and wife, except to me, it was master and property.

I remember music and dancing, though I didn't partake as much as was usual, my heart was not in it, and my stomach was elsewhere. The lovely banquet I scarcely touch and I hear the usual comment of nerves for her 'wedding night' that make my 'nerves' even worse and I have to excuse myself several times. Captain John hardly notices, and if he does, he says nothing to me.

He ate, he drank, he danced and made himself available to everyone in the room. A perfect gentleman, and when it is time to leave, he merely holds out his arm and escorts me away.

Our bridal room has been decorated with ribbons and flowers strewn everywhere. The huge double bed has clean, white sheets turned back. The curtains have been drawn and candles litter the room. On a small table near the window, a decanter with two glasses stands, along with a bowl of fruit and some small pastries. Captain John lets go of my arm, and walks over to the table, pours himself a large drink before turning to look at me.

I remain standing where he has left me, my back almost touching the locked door, surveying the room that would be witness to my torture. I feel his eyes on me and return the gaze; I lower my eyes first. He drinks thirstily and replaces the empty glass before walking purposefully towards me. He walks slowly around me, 'surveying his property from all directions'. I can say this for certain for those were his exact words.

"Strip."
I know I hear the word, but I don't quite register the meaning.
"Strip. I won't tell you again ... Wife."

He spoke 'wife' with such contempt I flinch at its venom but still don't move. I have not undressed myself since being old enough to wear corsets, and have no notion of how I would reach the small buttons, but besides that quandary was my reluctance to undress while he is watching. If he has to put his 'thing' near me then I will endure it as is expected of me, but this humiliation is not worthy of me.
I see that my incompliance to his demand causes him intense anger, but I will not be ordered by him. I deserve respect, even if I am merely his wife. I am wrong. Grabbing me by my shoulders, he pulls me towards him with such power, my hands fly up to his chest to steady myself.

His kiss is hard and vigorous. I almost gag at the feel of his hairy upper lip, and his thrusting tongue forces my own lips open, and invades my mouth. I can smell brandy and onions and I fight to move away. One of his hands moves down to my bosom, and begins massaging it fiercely, and causes me to squeal. He breaks off the kiss, breathing hard, and pulls at the front of my gown. It tears only slightly which frustrates him. He drags me to the bed and pushes me onto it front ways. I can feel his hot breath on my neck as he pulls at each beautifully crafted button and in his haste to get it off, he tears most of them.

Finally, he has me in nothing more than my corset, stockings and one shoe; the other has come off in transit to the bed. Flipping me onto my back, he undoes his trousers before climbing on top of me. I don't have time to see what will be hurting me, but I feel it knocking against my thighs as he pushes my legs wider apart.

At the same time, he is yanking down my corset to free my bosom. Suddenly he spits into his palm and rubs his hand between my legs on my ladies' parts. I find this so revolting I try to squirm away but he holds me flat, and begins prodding me again with his thing.

After a while he gives a triumphant grunt while I cry out in agony as he enters me. I try to move away, but he holds me fast and prods even more, pushing his thing further. It feels like I am on fire inside, and the tears I have held onto all day cascade down my cheeks, as the varying sensations continue. His heavy hand grips my bosom while his lower half pushes against my nether regions, causing excruciating agony until finally he lets out a cry, and goes limp above me, before rolling off.

I lie un-moving, not daring to, as every inch of my lower flesh throbs in pain, and my breasts feel sore and bruised. I listen to his heavy breathing that eventually turns into a snore, and only then do I roll over, wincing with each movement.

Something between my legs feels sleek, blood I suspect, remembering Katherine's embarrassed lesson on what to expect. I gingerly touch myself and stare at my blood stained fingers, but also something else. I sniff tentatively and recoil in disgust, wiping whatever it is on the already soiled bed sheet, and limp to the bathroom adjacent to the bedroom.
In the better light I am able to conduct a thorough inspection of myself. I gag at whatever he deposited inside me and wash quickly to be rid of its stench. Then I sit on the floor and let the tears fall. I could not consider the possibility that both my mother, and Katherine, have endured this on their wedding nights, and continue to suffer such violation. They both look happy and show affection towards their husbands. I know Katherine adores David and waited impatiently to have his children.

No, they must have experienced something else, something right and pure and loving. I have no notion what Captain John has done to me but I can say with all positivity, it is not love. I write this anxiously, expecting him to wake and find me, but so far, he has not and I have been left alone all these hours since his attack on my body. I pray that it is over.

April 24th 1853

It has been days since writing. I've considered it on many occasions, but to be frank, I have barely been left alone. Besides, I know he is watching me, and I refuse to allow him to know my mind. He has taken my body, but my thoughts he shall never have. I hide my diary from any prying eyes in a secret place within my luggage. I am positive that he knows nothing of my writings.

We are back from our 'honeymoon' in
Paris. I saw very little of it, and so
cannot share any wondrous sights,
beyond that our hotel was lovely. If I had
been there with anyone else I know I
would have enjoyed it immensely. As it
is, I was with my husband. I hope within
that sentence you can hear the contempt
in my writing. 'Husband' is merely
another title for owner, beater, brute,
evil, bully.
People looking at him regard Captain
John as an attentive husband, fussing
around his timid new wife. He smiles, he
talks, at least to others, to me he barely
passes the day, and that suits me fine, but
as the evening draws nearer, I see the
look in his eyes and know what is coming.

He found me later that night sitting on
the bathroom floor, clean of him and
crying. He pushed me to the floor and
repeated his previous actions, only this
time he pushed harder and further,
which caused me excruciating pain, but
his hand clamped over my mouth stifled
my screams.

Thankfully it didn't last long, and he collapsed on top of me with a groan. He left me there to clean myself up and I remained there till morning.

Six nights have been the same. He invades me, sometimes twice in one night and then behaves as though everything is normal during daylight. Thankfully the bruising left behind after his 'attacks' can be hidden by my dress, though a small bruise on my neck needs extra care, and I have to wear a high neck outfit, with Mothers pearls, which feels like I am being strangled again.

I accept the congratulations and smile through the afternoon tea Mother planned on our return. I believe that I convey myself as content, if perhaps a trifle anxious new wife, which I believe society deems acceptable. I speak of Paris as if I had seen enough of it, remaining vague but sharing what trips I hoped to take, and behaving as though I had triumphed in these outings. I must be convincing as nobody questions my imprecision on facts, and good manners would deem it unnecessary to question me further, and of this one behaviour I am eternally grateful.

Captain John watches me carefully, though he does it so well, that I'm not sure at first if I am under his scrutiny. I catch his eye on me once too often to be mistaken and realise that he has always watched me thus, but in my innocence I have refused to bear it. Now as his wretched 'wife' I am becoming accustomed to his behaviour, I am aware of him. He behaves accordingly with both parents and friends, who have been invited to welcome back the 'happy couple', and wave us off to my new home. Captain John's country house is ten miles from my parent's home where I grew up safe and secure. It is further away from town, and a little secluded. I am writing in what has been allocated as my own parlour, though in truth, he frequents it whenever he chooses, so in essence it is not my own, but only mine when he is absent.

Today he is gone. I know not where, nor care, for that matter. My courses began last night which repulsed him enough to leave me be, thankfully. He banished me out of our bedroom and bade me sleep elsewhere until I am deemed clean enough to share his bed. I have never before rejoiced at my monthly curse. Now, if they do indeed repulse him so, I shall look upon them as a monthly reprieve from his advances. If he despises them so badly I will endure them every day to stop his body touching my own.

April 27th 1853

My mother visits this morning and broaches the subject of offspring, to which I inform her of my courses starting. I see the disappointment in her eyes, before she quickly turns to pour the tea and I feel such anger towards her I almost speak out of turn. I manage to hold my tongue and abruptly change the focus onto more neutral subjects such as the garden that I consider needs attending.

I have spoken with the gardener as to what could be done to make it more pleasing. Mother seems satisfied with me. I pass lunch absentmindedly, nibbling on cheese and grapes whilst grimacing at the cramping pain that accompanies my courses, but today I do not cry with pain. Today I feel the sting of tears and hope that I'll be free for another few days at least. I spend the afternoon wandering around my new prison, picking up his bits and pieces, fingering his books, his art, his furniture and make mental notes of what I will change and add if I care enough; however, I do not. This is Captain John Harrison's home; it would never be mine, no matter how long I have to live in it.

He returns at dusk. Although he'd ridden out on his favourite horse, 'Jet' he returned on foot, possibly due to his being quite inebriated. His butler, Morris informs me of his return as I sit reading in the library, wondering if I should bother dressing for dinner alone. My stomach knots in anxiety and all thoughts of food flee my mind while I wait for him to appear.

April 28th 1853

I write my entry the morning after Captain John's return. I have scrubbed myself this morning until my skin is sore, especially my hands. I remember my elation that I may be free of him a week of every month, but it seems Captain John has learned of other ways to find his pleasure that involves my body. It's a quiet dinner of which I barely touch, while he wolfs his down hungrily. He watches me with a look of contempt and then he smiles. It makes me feel so uncomfortable I am glad when dinner is over and I can retire to my parlour; I am wrong. He follows me, and locks the door.

What occurs next is unfathomable to my mind, and yet now, the morning after such vulgar behaviour, I am innocent no longer, and can only convey my abhorrent feelings to the acts my husband demanded of me using my hands and bosom so that he did not go without his gratification.

He laughs at me when I retch at having his 'thing' so close to my face, and I recoil from it, but after holding me down and demanding I lay still, it is thankfully over in seconds, and I roll onto my side and do indeed vomit what little food I consumed. This angered him, and he stormed out once he dressed enough to be decent if seen by any of the servants.

I remain on the floor, turned away from my own puddle where I have deposited a stinking handkerchief that I used to mop up his residue. I make a mental note to burn it once I have the courage to wipe up after him. I just found the strength to move to the chair beside the fireplace, when he returns, a glass of port in his hand. He set this down, and stands before me, a smile playing on his lips, but I merely stare back at him and wait for the next assault on my body.

He reaches down and takes my right hand, and he places it on his groin area. I impulsively pull away, but he pushes my hand harder against himself, and begins to move against my rigid hand.

After a while, he lets go and my hand falls away. I am grateful thinking it is over, when he unbuttons his trousers and brings it out.

I have never seen it in the darkness, or candle-lit bedroom, and am thankful for that. Even during his last assault, I kept my eyes closed whilst wishing it to be over. It is rigid, long, pink and foul and I find it difficult to ponder how Mother, and Katherine, could tolerate such an object invading their bodies. I find no pleasure in it. But they behave as if a union between a man and woman is a wonderful act. This thing in front of me is what connects a male and female, and I find nothing pleasurable in its appearance and turn my face away. He reaches out for my hand again, and he places it on himself and warns me to hold it, and to do so gently, or else. I consider at that point if touching it hard would hurt him, or remove it permanently.

For now, I do as he demands and let him use my hand for his pleasure. He makes strange noises and pushes against my rigid arm, until I felt it go limp in my hand, and I release it. Holding my hand before me, I quickly leave the parlour, almost running upstairs to the bowl of water in my room, and I scrub my hand and arm clean. I will repeat this action again to be sure I have no trace of him on my skin.

May 7th 1853

It has been over a week since I last recorded my life on paper. This is not due to my idleness but that I have barely had a moment's peace. Within two days of my last writing, Captain John was hailed north to catch up with his regiment. I was able to fathom that his commanding officer likes my husband to be near him, and Captain John dares not refuse to indulge such a needy little man.

I cannot comprehend how such a man commands an army of others when he whines and complains so much. Lord George Paget, though I have not had the chance to meet with him myself due to his absence at the wedding, I am told he is a brave man, though a trifle unusual by some, but so far, I can only gain insight from what I overhear. It seems Lord George Paget is a rather complicated gentleman, and in my eyes, blind, if he enjoys Captain John's company. Of course, my husband does not 'attack' Lord Paget or humiliate him – I gather that his opinion would change if he knew.

Now, perhaps you think as I did, that I would be free to be myself during his absence. My presence was not required, or desired by all accounts. It seems I am wrong to think that I might have privacy. Captain John considers his absence from his new bride to be an upsetting ordeal for me, and has made arrangements for me to visit with his parents, and his cousins, who are staying awhile. My objections are never considered by himself. If anything, they're dismissed immediately and regarded as pointless.

The same day he departs, I am packed off to his parent's country estate on the Wiltshire borders.

Besides the journey being tedious, long and uncomfortable my feelings on the matter reach boiling point, and I scream into a clean handkerchief. During a stop to rest I flounce away and stomp up a small hillock, much to the concern of the carriage driver. He insists on following me, which beats the object of my walking away, but the exertion helps a little and I continue the journey resigned to my fate. During the ride, my thoughts tumble out of me like water. Memories and conversations I am able to recall in great detail. I felt something akin to this on my wedding day. I was resigned to do my duty for my parent's sake, regardless of my own thoughts and feelings on the matter. Now here I am again, being a good and obedient wife, going to a household I have no fondness for, merely because he has demanded it. Is my life to be so?

Again my thoughts refer back to the only women I can compare my situation to, and nothing is similar. I watch them closely when we meet and they show no signs of loathing or discomfort around their husbands. I know my father to be a kind man, and can never in all my life consider him to be a cruel man in public or in their private chambers, and the same with David. Katherine is content to carry another of his children, and smiles when with him. David is always attentive to her. I cannot contemplate that he could be so good an actor as my own husband. Their love has to be real.

And there is a word that makes no sense to me. Duty. I have married out of duty because my parents saw it as a good match. I lie un-moving on my bed, and let my husband do whatever he wishes to do, because it is my duty as a wife. Is that love? I heard that word frequently before my wedding day and hear it still from him, but what is duty? Is this my life now, to be dutiful to everyone but myself? Is it my duty to love Captain John Harrison? But how does love happen?

I arrive to a flurry of excitement from people and dogs, and am thankfully escorted to a quiet room at the back of the house that overlooks their grounds. The journey has made me feel quite nauseous and light-headed, so I am glad of the little respite. A modest, waist high maze takes most of the space, but the borders of the garden flourish in a multitude of colour, and I wish to walk outside in the fresh air, and clear my head. In the middle of the maze stands a small rectangular folly that catches my attention, as two children, a boy and a girl, run around it, laughing and shouting to each other. The nurse standing near-by gazes into the distance.

I guess them to be the twins of Anne who has married Captain John's brother, Richard. The children did not attend the wedding due to them having colds, but they seem much revived now, judging from their exertion.

I found myself dithering, enjoying the quiet of the room, and needing to wander the grounds in peace; but inevitably there is a knock at my door and a maid conveys the message that Sir George and Lady Gloria Harrison will entertain me in the front room when I am ready. Society knows that means: 'we are waiting to pour the tea so hurry down and don't keep everyone waiting longer than you have already'. I thank her and sigh loudly. The peace and quiet will have to wait. I am expected.

My entry is met by a group of people, including his parents whom I detest, as they always look down at my belly as if their staring will produce an heir.

Captain John's brother, Richard, glances at my chest as he bows to me. His petite wife Anne, a cousin from London called Rodney, and his friend, Luke Babbledon who stares openly at me, causing me to blush.

Thankfully the two children come running in, and are introduced as Milly and Markus before rushing out again, helping themselves to a biscuit as they pass the small table.

Four dogs of various breeds and size lick and sniff me, and a black cat lies watching me from the safety of the back of an armchair.

Thus begins a whirlwind of visits to various places, and people, dinner parties and lunches. I am barely left alone for a minute, and crave each time I need the chamber pot, and bedtime, for those are the only moments I gain any chance to catch my breath. I only see Betsy during these brief moments and I miss her familiar face terribly during the day. I tell her so and we hug briefly. I am so exhausted or suffering with a headache, that I cannot write a thing, and carefully conceal my diary before I fall asleep.

Days drag by in boredom, and each day is harder and harder to keep my face placid. I want to be free as I was only months ago.

May 11th 1853

My visit is over. My hell is not. Captain John travels down to his parent's home with this Lord George Paget as a surprise to his family, and myself. We are having afternoon tea on the lawn, whilst watching Milly and Markus attempt to play croquet. Luke has asked if I want to play, but I have a headache, and prefer the shade. I feel a sense of regret, but my head wins over any other thoughts on the matter.

Suddenly, unannounced, there he is, my husband and his friend. His father jumps up, as does Gloria; I do not move, nor say a word – it does not go un-noticed. I pay for my lack of affection. Following dinner, I cannot bear my head any longer, and excuse myself. This is apparently deemed unacceptable, but I ignore the horrified looks and whispered comments and retire to my room.

An hour later, Captain John follows me and demands to know of my indifferent behaviour towards his friend. It does not matter what I say. I think I mumble something about a migraine, but it is lost in his attack on me. Once he has finished, he leaves me there to return to the party below.
Today, we travel home.

May 13ᵗʰ 1853

I cannot tell you at this moment if I am happy or sad. I am happy to leave his parent's prison, without a doubt, but sad that I return to my own hell. From my visit, of two things I am positive: Anne does not love her husband, and Luke is appalling at hiding his feelings towards me.
I write this without pride or self-importance but throughout my visit I caught him looking at me.

Now, my experience of men looking was not a pleasant one, but I found myself hoping to find him staring, and I was never disappointed.

He is nearer my age, early twenties if he is the same age as Rodney, Captain John's cousin. Luke is tall, lean and has no moustache to hide his face. Instead he has quite prominent cheekbones that would make most ladies swoon with jealousy, that a man could possess such curves and not be a female. His grey eyes sought me out on every occasion and managed to follow up with simple chatter about nothing untoward or improper. I believe he was as much aware of other eyes watching him, as I was, and Luke is a true gentleman, giving no cause for a scandal.

Of Anne I will allow a moment of arrogance, in that, a woman who hates her husband can only be sure of another woman's abhorrence to her own partner as it is akin to watching oneself in a mirror.

I saw her recoil as he brushed the back of her neck absentmindedly during conversations, though she thought herself safe. Her acting abilities did not match my own, and for her own sake, I glance around the room to be sure no one else notices her loathing. I feel a small sense of connection to her, but no friendship can flourish under such circumstances. Captain John has been out for most of today with Lord Paget. I believe it is some military business, but to be frank, I wasn't listening. The headache I had two days ago, grew worse as we journeyed home, following his attack on my body. Of that night, I prefer to forget, as the torture I endured was inconceivable.

May 14th 1853

*I am not off the hook. Captain John and
Lord Paget are off again, and so I am to
visit my parents for a week of endless
dinner parties, as acquaintances of
Mother's want to catch up on how
married life treats me. Thankfully, the
journey is not a long one, and I arrive
before dinner, long enough to have a
bath, a true indulgence, and tonight will
be a fairly quiet affair, with two local
families joining us. Katherine is confined
now, so will not be with us.*

May 16th 1853

*Today Mother and I visit Katherine. She
looks uncomfortable, and big, and all I
can think is, that could be me if Captain
John has his own way, which he
inevitably will. We talk of names and
hopes, and my niece climbs over all of us,
with her nanny watching nearby.*

I love my little niece, Mary, but my nerves are on edge, and I feel bad-tempered and hot. I say as much to Katherine and she grins - apparently she felt much the same when pregnant with Mary. Her and Mother exchange looks, and I feel sick.

May 20th 1853

Finally I return to Captain John's house, and have a day and night of bliss. Betsy senses my need for being alone and hurries through her chores before leaving me in peace. No visitors, no parties, no husband. I wake to a flurry of excitement, as Morris has received a letter informing him of Captain John's return later today and I am required to organise a celebratory meal with cook. Finally, after a lot of time wasting, for both of us, I leave her to it, knowing she'd do a better job of organising a dinner, plus, she cares about her master, I do not. He can eat bones and choke for all I'd be concerned.

May 21st 1853

*I sit here alone. I have cried for so long,
my eyes hurt, but I have no more tears. I
hurt down below and bleed from a cut. I
move to get into a more comfortable
position.*

*Captain John returned home late and is
fed almost immediately once he's cleaned
up and changed. He enquires about my
visit with my parents, but there is no real
interest behind the question. It dawns on
me then that all those months of visits to
my parent's home, the dinner parties and
dances had all been false on his part. He
did not care for them or me. And for
what? I can only think that it was to win
their trust in handing over their
youngest daughter. I am merely a hole
for him to stick his thing inside, and a
bag to carry his heir. Surely any woman
will do?*

*He came to me as Betsy is helping me out
of my dress. Ordering her to leave, he
stands close to me, almost touching as he
stares down into my face. I know he sees
only contempt. I don't bother to hide it
anymore. It makes him laugh out loud.*

He undresses very slowly and carefully, making the moment last as long as possible. Reaching for my unresisting hand, he makes me hold his thing while he pushes against me. After a while, he tells me to let go, and he pulls me roughly to the bed. Throwing me onto my stomach, he lifts my chemise and thrusts into me from behind, whilst whispering the words, "you are my bitch, and so I shall take you as one."

Are all men like this? I can never believe my father is such, nor David who has no qualms in showing his affection towards my sister. What about Luke? Is he another tyrant hiding behind grey eyes and cheekbones? And what of Richard and Anne? Did he abuse her body as Captain John insists he has the right with mine? I can too easily imagine it, and cringe at such violence that could produce two innocent children, who are pleasant, if a little unruly. I can barely contemplate such a hateful act, and then having to bear his children. I pray silently for my courses.

May 28ᵗʰ 1853

My nephew is born in the early hours of this morning, Andrew David Edgeworthy. Katherine is doing well and I am informed that all are happy and healthy. I cry for hours.

May 29ᵗʰ 1853

All my hope is lost. My courses are late, and I feel nauseous. I fear the worst. Captain John did resume his husbandly rights from the moment he returned. It seems taking my body like a dog, has become his favourite position of humiliation. It has left me bruised and sore, and I bathe most mornings in lavender to try and ease the discomfort, though by nightfall his penetrations cause more sores, so I am fighting a losing battle.
If I am indeed pregnant, it may give me time to recuperate, as surely he will not expect to have me during a pregnancy?

I will wait though, a few more days. I could be wrong. I cannot fathom which to pray for. Pregnancy which may ease his attention on my body, but the very idea of carrying his child is appalling to me. Or do I hope that he has failed again, which gives me some semblance of pleasure that my body denies his child, but then the attacks will continue.

June 5th 1853

I informed Captain John of my pregnancy last night after dinner. He stood motionless whilst staring into the fire before leaving the room without any word. Later, he came to our bedroom. I could smell the alcohol on him long before he climbed into bed. I curled up as far away from him as was possible, as always wishing that the bed was bigger or better yet, in another room away from his body. He curled up behind me and gently rubbed my stomach. He spoke words that were barely coherent, before passing out and I am finally left alone.

I woke this morning with an odd feeling; my body has not been assaulted, though my mind has been. If I am to be honest, it is the closest act of affection I have been offered by Captain John. His gentle rubbing on my stomach, though he did not ask permission to do so, has been a show of satisfaction that I have done my duty finally as his wife, and now carry his child. It is all I have time to contemplate before I bolt for the chamber pot, and vomit what little I have inside me. My noises wake him and he abruptly leaves the room, pulling on his dressing gown as he goes. I hear him shouting for Betsy, who appears bleary-eyed and takes the pot away.

His parents are informed immediately, as are my own. We receive a telegram within the hour that they will be arriving later this evening to celebrate, and preparations are made to accommodate everyone. The house is at this moment alive, and bustling with activity, as rooms are prepared and food bought for a lavish meal. I have had my orders to rest, and Betsy and cook will see to everything. In truth, I am grateful for it.

June 10th 1853

As I write, let it be plain that I am still in shock at what transpired. Captain John's conduct changed dramatically towards me following my announcement. He has been attentive, concerned, and dare I say, kind, careful of my condition and making certain of my comfort. I respond with suspicion at first, but as my courses do not show, I begin to realise that pregnancy will be my respite.
I gradually relax and take some pleasure in his attention. Though love is an emotion I doubt I will ever feel for him, I have not felt frightened or anxious throughout my days. Instead I am lavished with presents, and sweetmeats, to tempt my appetite.
The physician has confirmed that I am in the early stages of pregnancy and that the sickness should abate soon. I sleep a lot, and when not sleeping or vomiting, I am eating or strolling slowly around the garden, watching the gardener make the garden more appealing, and he is doing a fine job.

June 17th 1853

I believe I feel a small, hardness beneath my navel. This is his child growing. I cannot fathom at this moment how I feel about it. Katherine came today with my new nephew, Andrew. He is so tiny, and I fear holding him, but Katherine insists. She is looking surprisingly well considering, and wants to congratulate me on my pregnancy, despite David's concerns to her travelling.
Andrew's nurse, who hovers nearby, places Andrew in his basket while we sit on a rug on the lawn. Katherine can barely keep her focus on me as we talk about this and that. We chat mostly regarding my own coming child, and how to cope with the almost constant nausea that I suffer. Betsy told me about eating ginger, and so far, this has helped enormously. I was telling Katherine about keeping a small piece by my bedside when Gloria arrives and takes over the conversation, informing me that it would be best for me to stay inside, in case the slight chill harms my son.

I hear Katherine's intake of breath, as did Gloria who gives her a foul look of contempt, before ordering the maids to clear away the rug and I am to be helped inside. I do not know what it was that made me speak, but I did.

"I do not wish to go inside on such a fine, warm day and do not consider yourself a god, Lady Harrison, as to know the sex of my child before it is even born to me." I emphasise the word, 'my' and turn away to hide my crimson cheeks. I hastily sit on my hands to hide the shaking, and wait for the onslaught - none comes. Lady Harrison storms away.

Katherine is horrified at my impertinence but I say nothing to defend myself. How dare she decide where it is I sit. My husband has a right to order me around, but I'll be damned if his mother does the same. We remain sitting outside for another hour or more, and ask for tea and cakes to be brought out.

Katherine eventually leaves, giving me a tight hug and a knowing smile. She knows as well as I that someone will reprimand me. When we sit down for dinner, Gloria does not look at me, or engage in any conversation with me. Captain John says nothing either - the meal is long and awkward, but I am never going to apologise to that beastly woman.

June 20th 1853

My mother arrives unannounced this afternoon. I am resting in my room. The weather is so hot and uncomfortable, that it is making the nausea worse and only the coolness of my bedroom with the windows wide open can alleviate my symptoms so far. Of course, there is also the additional benefit of not having to see Gloria whom I am aware that etiquette requires me to call her Lady Harrison, and I do in public, but in these pages, she is no lady to me, merely a pest.

With regards to my mother, she is
fretting that my pregnancy is causing
my manners to fail me and that must
never happen, especially to 'Lady
Harrison', (Mother's words, not mine). I
see Katherine still reports back to our
parents; shame really. It seems I really do
not have a true friend or confidante in
this world, except Betsy, but even with
her, I am aware of class and what is
correct.

I am fearful for Betsy. The family
allowed her to come with me, but for how
long? My pregnancy will hopefully
postpone any ideas of relieving her of this
job, however, I am aware that Betsy was
my one demand to my mother and it was
granted – for now.

I inform Mother that Gloria can apologise
to me whenever she is ready, but I'll be
damned before I go to her, for I have done
nothing wrong. Unless of course, sitting
on one's lawn is now wrong?

Mother cannot answer such a ridiculous question, and we fall silent while she gets up and wanders around the bedroom. Finally, Mother moves onto other subjects, such as, Father and his business in the city. He is planning on staying in London for a few days. Mother is inviting a few of her oldest friends down for the summer. One lady, Veronica, lives in Cheshire, and she has extended the invitation for Mother to return with her for a holiday until autumn. Mother was indecisive on the matter, but I convince her that it will be good for her, and besides, the baby isn't due until early spring.

Mother leaves and I relax a while, enjoying the warm breeze that touches my skin like a soft caress. I must have dozed, for I wake with a start, to find Captain John watching me from the doorway. The look he gives me is one I cannot fathom, and I ease myself upwards, and get out of bed. I pull the bell for Betsy to come and dress me for dinner, and with a slight bow, he turns and leaves me. No words have been spoken, but I feel ill at ease.

June 25th 1853

The weather is stiflingly hot and it is difficult to get comfortable. The nausea continues, though abates for a few hours when I nibble on ginger and dry biscuits; these are my constant companions now. Captain John has taken to sleeping in his own bedroom further down the hall, to allow me freedom to move around in the bed and get comfortable in this heat. I must admit to feeling surprise at such consideration, but he is merely looking for his own comfort. Nobody wants to be near another sweating body. Certainly not one that moves about almost constantly, and uses the chamber pot every hour, which only brings on the nausea, and sleep becomes nothing more than a wish. I am exhausted.

During the day I rest, or take a leisurely stroll around our garden which is transforming nicely. Even Captain John came out and admired it the other day and congratulated the gardener for his efforts. I sit for a while on one of the two benches that are either side of the lawn, and enjoy the feel of the sun through my dress, until Captain John sees me and orders me back inside. I allow him to escort me in, but I cannot settle, and wander around the house.

I feel uneasy, though I cannot explain it. The child is growing, I can feel the shifts within my body and it is tiring me. I feel nothing for this child; which frightens me, as surely I should feel something. For is it not part of me also? I sit for hours contemplating such feelings, and know that my lack of any comes from how this child was created - through pain and hatred. How can I love such a creature that comes only through my own suffering?

I have considered going to church, to beg forgiveness from Mary, a mother, the mother of us all, and yet, whenever we go to church, I feel only a deep sadness and I feel even more alone. As if the church is another reminder that I am beholden to this man I hate, whom God is allowing to hurt me, merely because I am a woman.

July 1st 1853

My relationship with Captain John has indeed changed. He is attentive to my every need and has not touched me in any way, other than holding my hand and kissing it, which I can bear. The nausea has diminished slightly, and I only feel sick early in the morning, and if I smell fish.

Captain John ordered that no fish be served until I feel able; I am grateful for his compassion and say as much. I think he appreciated my saying so, and we have a bearable evening together, with family and friends who come to celebrate Sir George's birthday. Captain John wanted to hold it here; who am I to argue.

The heat continues and I am glad for the first time that we are in the countryside, near a town and not in the cities. According to the newspapers, London stinks, as the Thames dries, and the stench of rotting meat and sewage reaches far and wide. My father returned last week, and spoke of it over dinner. He said ladies were fainting from the heat and the rancid smells, and people's odours were rife. I admit to thanking whoever was listening, that I lived in Sussex. London, I find, is a great city to visit, but I do not think that I could live there permanently.

Today I walk a little around the nearby park. It is no more than a slow stroll, to be out of the house and gardens that have begun to feel like my prison. Everyone watches me for signs of any problems. If Captain John is home, he questions me about my needs, and I feel cocooned sometimes. It is nice to feel free and alone. I know of course, that this is highly irregular, but I don't care.

I watch the swans and ducks fighting over mere crumbs thrown in by a governess and her charge. I listen to the chatter of the birds and the soft hum of conversations as people stroll by, some arm in arm, the aura of love surrounding one couple and I feel a stab of jealousy. I am eighteen years of age, pregnant, with my whole life ahead of me, and yet the life I see is one I feel nothing for, but dread.

I am resting on one of the many benches that litter the park when I hear my name. Turning towards the voice, my heart begins to beat faster, and something strange and unfamiliar happens within my body, as Luke Babbleton walks towards me.

He removes his hat, bows and asks to sit beside me. I am aware of my cheeks burning, and I become flustered and unsure of myself as he sits next to me. I have never sat with a man besides my father and husband, un-chaperoned, and I am not sure of the protocol.

Luke insists I call him by his first name and so it shall remain so. Even now, after the event, it feels a trifle, 'naughty', to be so forward in our address, but there it is; it is done now.

He asks after my wellbeing and congratulates me on my child. He speaks about London, and his father's business, and why he was visiting his uncle who it transpired lives but a few doors away from me. It seems the heat is causing problems for everyone, and Luke has escaped its confines and is breathing cleaner air here. He asks me about the forthcoming ball that is being held by his uncle, and if I'd be attending. I make some excuse about being careful with my pregnancy, but in truth, I knew nothing of such ball. He offers to walk me home and thinking it to be proper, I accept.

My return is met with barely contained self-control, when Captain John sees that Luke escorted me home. Luke leaves almost immediately, following a short conversation with Captain John, with regards to his parents' health and his brother. He mentions the ball again within earshot of me, bows and leaves, claiming a need to run errands.

I turned my back to walk into the cool library, when the tirade of accusations begins from my husband, regarding my conduct with Luke, and my deception to meet him secretly. He speaks of adultery and his expectations of my being here in his house. I dare not retaliate and withdraw to the drawing room. Captain John follows me and the accusations continue.

Something inside of me snaps. I cannot say what it was, but accusing me of an illicit affair after all the months of abuse that would deem such an act agreeable, and yet I am innocent, and his accusations are inexcusable and I tell him as much.

In that moment I tell him everything.
How much I despise him. How much he
sickens me and yet I remain faithful, and
why have I not been informed of the ball
of which we'd been invited?
I have the satisfaction of seeing his
expression of surprise followed by an
anger that swiftly follows and I abruptly
sit back in my chair. It is obvious to me
at that point, that no woman has ever
spoken back to him, certainly not a young
eighteen year old, regardless of my
position. He informs me, that he is master
of this house, and I am to obey him
regardless of my feelings towards him.
We are together till death, and he decides
if his wife will be attending any balls, or
dinner parties, and no, he will not permit
me in my condition, to frolic around at a
ball, and that was the end of that
conversation.

July 5th 1853

The last few days I have spent in silence for the most part. I am confined to the house and gardens with strict instructions to watch me when he has to leave on one errand or another, to do with his regiment no doubt. Sometimes he is gone for hours, returning with the smell of alcohol and perfume about his person, and I wonder where he has been, purely out of curiosity, not caring one way or the other.

It is Betsy who enlightens me on the type of house he is frequenting and that suits me fine. Though in truth, I am perplexed as to how a lady would allow a man to do what Captain John does. But having thought long about it, I concur that the poor woman may have no choice, and has to endure it purely for the money received. I sincerely hope that whoever she is that she is paid well. If he receives his pleasure there, then surely I will become irrelevant, and can live my own life?

Captain John has barely spoken with me, or looked at me since my outburst, and this suits me fine. He may think that he is punishing me, but if truth be told, I am completely at my ease without any conversations with him. My opinion of him remains. Captain John is incapable of being a decent human being.

He came to my bed sometime in the early hours and woke me from my sleep. He was drunk and had obviously forgotten that he now sleeps in his own room – and why he chose to do that. I woke with a start to feeling his hand on my breast, grasping and fondling so hard, I cried out. I receive a sharp blow across my face for making a noise and he hisses in my ear to 'shut up'.

I curl into myself, my face on fire, trying to keep myself safe, but he does nothing else. He eventually stood, a little unsteadily, and looks down at me for a moment, before stumbling out of the bedroom, leaving the door wide open. I quickly jump out of bed and shut it, there was no key to lock it; Captain John has taken it with him.

July 11th 1853

I lose his child. I begin bleeding heavily early this morning. I wake to agonising pain. Captain John has not returned from one of his 'visits' and it is dearest Betsy who organises towels, clean linen and hurries Morris to fetch the doctor. He came too late, and something was born to me, but I was not allowed to see it. Captain John arrives to a bustling household, and an exhausted wife. When he is informed, he apparently weeps and goes in search of some comfort in the decanter with the doctor, who leaves him there, before departing for his breakfast.

Captain John's child is taken away while I am duly cleaned and fussed over. I let them do whatever they want. I feel numb. My feelings towards Captain John's child were just that, nothing; it had been his, not mine. I played no part in its creation, merely a place to hold it, until it ripped me to shreds as its father had done putting it in there.

To you I may seem heartless and cold. I do not deny this, nor will I defend myself on this matter. His child is gone. My barrier against his assaults has gone. I feel only a creeping fear and revulsion, but of grief, I feel nothing.

As I write these words I can hear Captain John downstairs, he is drunk. He is shouting incoherent words followed by crying. I hear something smash against the library wall and a subsequent check by Morris who is duly dismissed for the night. Betsy has already informed me that Morris has ordered all staff to stay away from the library regardless of what they hear. The master is grieving and shall not be disturbed.

July 12th 1853

I sleep restlessly since the baby died yesterday morning. Doctor Hobson returned twice to check on my well being and informs me that there should be no reason why another pregnancy will not be possible, and will tell Captain John the same news.

I implore him to also add that he is to
leave me for a while to heal, and he
consents, agreeing that it would be for
the best if I allow a week or more to heal
physically, and as long as I need to grieve
and heal emotionally.

This last statement I know is directed
towards me alone with regards to my
lack of bereavement. I know the staff
whisper about my lack of tears in this
matter, Betsy has told me, but I cannot
force anything from my eyes. My heart
feels empty, as does my womb and I know
my reprieve will be short-lived.

July 13th 1853

I was interrupted in last night's writings
as Captain John invaded our bedroom in
a drunken roar. He pushed his face so
close to mine, the stench of brandy
wafting into my senses. He condemned
me for killing his child, and never
wanting it, and warned me that this
would not be the last time he would fill
my belly.

I had best make peace with it, as he intended for us to have many children to carry on his family name, regardless of my feelings on the matter. He left bidding me a good night for he would heed Doctor Hobson's instruction to allow me to heal for a week and then he would resume his husbandly duties with a vengeance.

Since that moment I have wept so many times my eyes are flushed red and swollen. The staff, believing it to be delayed grief have rallied round and are doing everything they can to comfort me. Only Betsy knows the true reason for my tears, but what comfort can she give me as the days count down and my body begins to mend?

Both my mother and Katherine visit today and attempt to console me. How can I tell them it is not his child I grieve, but my own torment that will come? They would not heed me before this marriage and Mother made it plain that she is not concerned with my feelings on the matter of being Captain John Harrison's wife.

Father made the decision, sure in his knowledge that the marriage would be beneficial for both families. Mother will never go against his decision. I am alone.

July 19th 1853

Almost a week has passed and my body does indeed heal, much to my horror. I am able to walk further and the uncomfortable soreness has lessened greatly for which I am truly grateful, as I have never experienced such tenderness in all my days and would hope to never again. I have fought every emotion whilst recuperating from this loss. For the most part, I am confined to bed to allow the blood flow to ease, but I cannot rest, as I fret about the coming torture. My walking is also my reminder of his violation on what is private and should be respected. I fear the whole household know of my shame; Betsy pleads innocence on the matter.

I also feel the need to write, as I am unable to voice my dishonour that people assume my swollen eyes are for the child. I cannot correct them in their assumption. I let them all believe the lie. I despise myself for such a falsehood, but I can think of no alternative. To convey the truth of it, would I am sure, encourage such negative emotions and retorts from everyone, including Mother that our relationship may never mend. Whilst I yearn to be honest with Mother, I prefer to have a relationship with her, and so the deception continues. Besides, although I feel alone, I am aware of people's kindness and concern for my wellbeing, and I yearn for such loving gestures, more than I can say, so I continue to believe my own lie.

The one person whom I do not have to pretend with is Captain John. He barely acknowledges my presence and for that I am truly grateful. His lack of concern for me is also changing people's perception of him, especially the staff, who Betsy tells me, are appalled at his coldness.

My week is over, and tonight fills me with such dread and anxiety I feel myself clinging onto my mother as she climbs into her carriage. She turns surprised, but with a little pat, I am released and she leaves me. Now I wait.

July 20th 1853

When Mother left yesterday afternoon, I lived in torment the rest of the day, but Captain John did not come to our bedroom. I think this is his new torture, as waiting for his attack was more terrifying than the actual abuse. He was not home when Mother left, and did not return until the early hours, at dawn apparently. I had fallen asleep from sheer exhaustion by this time.

Doctor Hobson's visit this morning cleared me of any ill health, declaring I am strong and being young, I would conceive again. The bleeding is minimal and I don't feel as weak as I had.

He enquires about my mourning period as the child could not have been more than 10 weeks carried. Betsy has already organised a dress to suit society - I have not even considered it until she brought it up, regarding purchasing a new black outfit to mourn my child.

He orders me out of the house, to stroll gently and exercise. I would have danced around the room, if I were able. As it is, I shake his hand with as much enthusiasm as I can muster. He says that in his opinion, at around ten weeks, it is not considered a 'child' as yet. It has not fully formed, and so my mourning should be partial, which means that my wifely duties can continue.

I am left dumbstruck by his candid opinion and abruptly let go of his hand. He calls Betsy into the bedroom as he suspects that I am about to faint, but I assure him I am well. I thank him for his advice and assure him that I shall act upon his counsel immediately. Morris is informed of my exercise, and once Doctor Hobson leaves, Betsy prepares me for outside. We head for the park, which is a very short stroll from the house.

We spend a very pleasant hour watching people, strolling around the flower beds and smiling at the swans and ducks. It feels so liberating to be away from his house. The city of London is but an hour's carriage ride away and from our bedroom window one can see the steeples and chimneys of the higher buildings, but I have not ventured there since I was a girl of sixteen. I voice my need to explore to Betsy, but she shrugs non-committal, and I understand why. Captain John.

We miss lunch, but my appetite is not as it used to be. I gained a little weight during the pregnancy, but not much. I know it will be easy to regain my old waistline, and yet, it doesn't feel as important. Tiny waists are achieved to attract a husband, I already have one. It is expected that I continue to look my very best, so as not to embarrass Captain John, but I feel indifferent with regards to that. It has been so long since I danced, since I smiled with real amusements, and felt light and free. My life is a drudge and would always be so with him.

My return from the park is met with hostility, as Captain John has risen from his bed in a foul mood at finding out his wife has gone out. He'd been informed of my stroll and Doctor Hobson's advice. Out of respect for the servants I withdraw to the bedroom to lie down and rest, expecting him to follow; he did. Captain John follows me and pushes me inside, slamming the door behind him. He shouts that he tells me where I can go and when, not Doctor Hobson, and I should be in mourning, and it is a disgrace ... I stopped listening after that.

My unresponsive silence was enough for him, though I believe that anything would have been sufficient excuse for the behaviour that followed. Captain John lunged at me. Too tired to react quickly, I felt like a rag doll as he pulled me roughly to my feet and shook me violently before pushing me to the floor. I bruise my arm and ribs, but worse still, it knocks the breath out of me, and I lie gasping as he quickly undresses.

I cannot convey even on paper what occurred in the hours that followed. I am left bruised and bleeding, covered in his stinking substance and cringing away from the acts he forced me to perform. I now knew the depths of depravity Captain John can sink to, and I wish myself dead.

July 24th 1853

I am now watched almost constantly, yet I feel so alone - how is that possible? Morris is unwell with some fever or other, as is most of the staff, including Betsy, who has retired to her bed. From what I understand this fever is spreading throughout the city. My only wish now is that I or Captain John catch it, and die, so that either my soul may rest or that my body may.

As it is I am ravished daily as promised, but worse for me are the acts of barbaric gross indecency that I am forced to partake in. Lately Captain John has used the threat of dismissing Betsy as leverage upon me, and I resign myself to his will. Days have gone by in a blur. I am aware that my mother enquires about my health, and has been placated by his lies. Invitations to balls and parties are not forthcoming, due to my mourning, and so I am alone - with him.

The truth is that he dares not allow anyone to witness my bruises, or risk my loose tongue in company. Stupid man knows me not, for what shame would I endure if it were known of my daily abuse. I never speak of it, not even to Betsy now. My mind refuses to consider it during the daylight hours, as if I need respite from the horror. My mouth shows an unwillingness to form the words that would explain exactly what it is I witness. As it is, merely writing it is causing me great anxiety, yet I force myself to write. The pages bear witness to his crimes, and for now, that is all I can hope for.

July 27th 1853

The fever took Morris and one of the
young scullery maids. Captain John
orders that we stay with his family in the
country awhile to escape the disease. He
is fearful that this illness will carry away
his young bride, or worse, a possible child.
It is not inconceivable that I may be
pregnant again. His parents invite him
home to their country estate where there
is no illness as yet.
With this in mind he does not assault me,
not from mercy, but to be sure that no
signs of his attacks are witnessed by
anyone. I do not bother to question his
motives in leaving, I only feel empty that
I have not caught whatever this illness is
and died. Death to me is my only escape
route, or perhaps better yet, his death.
There are rumours of war and Betsy, who
is up and about again, though coughing
profusely, is clever enough to listen in on
a conversation only yesterday, with
regards to Captain John returning to his
regiment on a more permanent basis, to
prepare for battle and train the men.

Elated I almost dance around the bedroom, until I remember myself, and merely smile at my reflection in the dressing table mirror.

July 29th 1853

I write from the confines of Captain John's parent's estate. The grounds are magnificent as is the house, but eyes are upon me at every turn, and so with less privacy, this may as well be another prison. Gloria barely speaks two words to me, and glances downwards at my abdomen with such contempt, before turning away and talking to someone else. I catch Sir George glancing downwards also, but in a more melancholic manner, as if his very stare can create a pregnancy. They do not ask of my wellbeing, nor show any empathy for my grief - though I feel none, it would be courteous to enquire - surely?

I finally confide in Betsy that I know nothing about babies, and with crimson cheeks I ask in a whisper, what his stinking substance is. Once she explained it, I am mortified, and have scrubbed myself clean following his last attack, visualising tadpoles, and despising such creatures near me. How repulsive, that a man holds such creatures, and it is expected that they should invade my body and produce his heir. I cannot fathom such ugliness.

We get word that Katherine's new born son, Andrew is very sick from this fever. I long to see her and to get away from the confines of this prison, but Captain John refuses to listen to my pleadings. She adores her children because she loves her husband, though in truth I still cannot understand how she would welcome his tadpoles?

I send word that I shall pray for them both, and make a pathetic excuse about not coming.

I hear that my mother and father were most upset at my absence, and point out that Katherine lives but half a day's ride, and what could possibly be more important that keeps me confined to Sir George's estate? I do not answer their telegram.

July 31st 1853

Andrew died.

August 1st 1853

I found it impossible to continue writing yesterday. My heart is heavy, even though I have only had the pleasure of meeting my nephew once; I feel considerable emotion for Katherine. I beg Captain John to allow me to be with her, but he insists on sending a telegram first. He refuses to allow me near any probable illness. At least, that is his excuse. I do not believe it for one moment.

So far I have not received word back from either my parents, or David, and so I am left in the dark, waiting to hear if my sister requires my company in her darkest hour. I wear a black dress as I mourn the perfect little boy who was loved.

I have to stop writing as a gardener abruptly appears in the large garden, looking sheepish, tipping his cap as he goes about pruning the nearby bush. I am not naive enough to believe that it actually needs pruning, but he's merely been given orders to hunt me down, and keep a close eye on me. I neatly pack away my things and drift off, aware that eyes follow my direction.

I write now from a stable stall, hidden from view by a rather large black and white horse. I am a little wary to be sure of such a creature, but I would rather take my chances with him than anyone at the house. Anne and Richard arrived without the twins.

Betsy has come to find me, and I reluctantly return to the house, whereupon, I attempt a conversation with Anne, who quietly tells me of her sadness at such a loss. I tell her that I held my nephew only once, and the conversation dies away, while our mother-in-law takes over all discussions, refusing to allow us even a moment to ourselves.

Gloria then insists that we should have no secrets within her house, and informs us that we must divulge all to her. I clamp my mouth shut, refusing to engage in such nonsense, of which she considers me rude. I look back at her defiantly, but remain silent. I glance across at Anne, who dutifully bows her head submissively and I know that this pathetic woman will never be someone I can trust.

"Now Anne is a true lady, worthy of this house." Gloria's voice is loud enough for all to hear.

I find this ridiculous remark so amusing I giggle, which catches the attention of everyone in the room, and I smile sweetly. Captain John is watching me closely from his position on the opposite side of the room. I give him such a look of contempt, I hope it will be noticed and commented on.

I sit quietly while a game of Bridge is played and listen to the usual chatter and gossip. Boredom sets in rather quickly and I excuse myself. I am half way up the stairs when I catch sight of Anne. She has followed me, I am sure, however, she hesitates in the shadows, and her indecisiveness costs us both dearly, as Richard steps out of the room and speaks quietly to her. I hear her mention the bathroom, and quickly step back further into the stairs so Richard will not see me. With a quick bow, he returns to the room, and with a brief glance up at me, Anne quickly follows.

I know in that instant that we are the same. Two women in loveless marriages, bearing the physical needs of our husbands, and I feel a pang of regret that she is not someone I can confide in. To bear such pain alone is beyond comparison, and I quietly send her a prayer.

August 3rd 1853

Two long tedious days pass and I have been unable to spend time alone with Anne. I catch Anne's gaze upon me on occasion and I smile back hoping to elicit some response, but she looks away and engages in conversation with everyone else. I find myself sitting on the outskirts of the room, watching them gossip, and I feel all the more detached from these people. They are of the same class and yet the more I sit and watch, the more I feel disinclined to associate myself with them.

I am studying them and am more than aware that they are examining me in return. I am conscious of whispers and abrupt changes of subjects as I enter the room along with malicious stares, and twisted faces, if I offer an opinion that does not reflect their own. I am meant to be in mourning, so is Captain John, but neither one of us behaves as such, at least not for his child. I because I cannot feel something akin to loss for an object thrust into me with such cruelty, and he, because he is arrogant and cruel. I do mourn dear little Andrew, but I refuse to voice this to these people.

Captain John's family are spiteful, revolting creatures of whom I want no part, yet I remain sitting in the chair, clasping a lukewarm, stewed cup of tea, and smile in all the right places, playing the dutiful wife, ignoring the glances at my belly and the hurtful looks that follow.

I have been blamed for losing the heir, and I am expected to rectify the matter sooner rather than later. That is my only role here, and with this in my mind, I can truly say that I despise my life. I also catch Richard staring at me in an odd fashion, that makes my skin crawl, and I immediately search for another human being to satisfy my safety.

I yearn for the old days, even this time last year I heard rumours of Captain John's intentions towards me, but I gave them very little thought. He was nothing more than a visitor to my parents and I was still free to be myself. I wonder now how much of that old me still exists. I loved to walk whenever I chose, not when my husband deemed it possible.

I enjoyed reading, yet every novel I attempt I lose interest and have replaced it in the book shelves un-finished. I loved to bake with Elsa, our old cook and housekeeper, who allowed me to have space within the kitchen on occasions.

We'd sit and eat my cake or pie afterwards, whilst passing the time of day. I enjoyed nature and would follow butterflies and dragonflies for hours in the summer. I missed my cats, Tabitha and Morgan who I found abandoned in one of the outer barns. I regret terribly the absence of life.

I miss Katherine dreadfully, and worry endlessly, but so far, I have not received word. I must admit that I am not convinced that word has not come; only that Captain John has not passed on the information to me. I know that a telegram arrived yesterday morning. I am stuck in this place, without comfort or friendship, and at Captain John's mercy during the nights.

August 6th 1853

We are returned to Captain John's house.
He deemed it safe to return and continue
life there. In truth, I believe he lost his
patience with his parents and brother
regarding his lack of heir. I also believe
he misses his whore. I believe this to be
true, as almost before the bags have been
removed from the carriage, he is away in
it. I am left to organise the servants, and
welcome the new butler, Mr Hargreaves
who has so far shown a cheery
disposition. He smiles where Morris
would merely look at you expectantly.
Mr Hargreaves is a little younger than
Morris, and we also have the pleasure of
his niece, Annabelle, who is being
employed as a seamstress and a between
maid.
I enquire as to their settling in and both
seem well adjusted and have taken to
their roles happily since our departure,
and look forward to working with us now
we're returned. I like them. Hargreaves is
widowed but of his wife's death I have no
knowledge, and his niece, Annabelle is
perhaps a few years younger than myself

She is petite, with a wide smile and bright blue eyes. Her willingness to show her skills are a trifle overwhelming, but I concur that a new gown would be agreeable and after deciding on a piece of green cloth, she leaves me with a smile. For the rest of the day I enjoy my own company, free of prying eyes, vicious tongues and naughty children. His abrupt leaving on our arrival, tells me that he is missing his pleasure with a willing partner. I merely behave as though I am dead, which I know he hates, but it is the only power I have.

August 8th1853

The household feels different with Hargreaves and Annabelle. Mrs. Martins is friendlier towards me. Although I am still in mourning, it is considered a half mourning, as the babe died so young in the pregnancy. They do not seem to judge me harshly if I take a stroll or visit the shops with Betsy.

Yes, I have ignored my husband's demands to remain within the confines of his prison. It is my rebellion against his behaviour. He cannot do worse to me than he already has. By stopping me from going to my own sister in her hour of need has shown me his depths, and I have survived them, though I do not know how to fix them.

Captain John is thankfully absent for most of the time since our return. I do not care where he goes, nor care whom he is with, so long as he is gone, though his return heralds another attack on my body.

Today, he receives a telegram that sends him into a terrible rage. Thankfully I am not in his presence but am downstairs with Annabelle, who is adding some finishing touches to my new gown. We both stop what we're doing on hearing his roar of anger, and don't move until we hear the front door slam. I immediately apologise to Annabelle, as I see her look of terror. I feel such shame.

On his return hours later I refuse to enquire as to his telegram and its contents. I know that my disinterest irritates him further, but I cannot muster the effort to lie and remain mute during dinner. I may not have any control over my life, but I can be in command of my mouth, and my facial expressions, and I make sure he sees every disgusted expression I can produce. It only enflames his fury even more, but it seems I have reached a point within myself that I don't care anymore. Married four months and I have learned nothing, beyond the fact that I am necessary to carry his heir. I do not think he sees me as a woman, but a belonging that has no worth beyond the obvious.

With dinner over, he disappears into his study where the brandy decanter can be found. I've been helping myself to small glasses of his brandy whenever he is absent, and I wait for the accusation, but none comes, I relax in my own parlor, staring at the fire, digesting another lovely meal.

Mrs. Martins, the cook here, has been adequate though sometimes her meals have been a little dry. Now that she has Annabelle to help her, the meals have tasted so much better, and I find my appetite again. I must admit to a sense of dread as I eat more than usual, and wait for my courses with trepidation.

August 11th 1853

Days have passed since I last wrote. Captain John has been out for the most part, sometimes all night, returning in the dawn hours and sleeping, if he is not engaged with officers of his company. A telegram arrived from his regiment and seems Captain John was not here to open it; I did, merely to check its importance. He has been summoned to his barracks to oversee the training of soldiers for an impending war. It seems Russia is not playing fair and the possibility of war is likely.

I dance around my parlour at such news. In truth, do not think of me as a heartless woman. I would not ask for a war that will kill many defenceless people, however, Captain John's absence is not to be taken lightly, and a large smile spreads across my face as I re-read the words. I feel a sense of hope that I might be free of these confines.

I take a stroll today in the park near our home, with Betsy, and Annabelle, as chaperones. It is nice, walking with girls my own age, if not class. Today is a glorious summer's day, and although the black garments are making me heat up quickly, I cannot be confined to his house. We had been walking for a while, when I see him in the distance, Luke Babbleton. He is watching our approach with a smile and as we near, Luke bows politely. He is helping a young boy with his boat on the lake, and introduces us to his nephew, Gilbert.

We then pass a very pleasant half hour, chatting about this and that. He heard of my nephew's death, and informs us of others who have died from the illness. Mainly elderly who are known to me, but I have not had the pleasure of their company. He does not mention my own child's death, and I am grateful for it. I find it difficult to be false within his company. To pretend to be grieving for something I felt only revulsion for, would be a tragedy. I like to believe that Luke and I are prepared to be honest with each other, within the confines of our society.

We are about to part company when Luke reaches out and takes my hand, kisses it, and asks me what I am doing for my birthday. I am so shocked by his touch I find it difficult to answer for a moment. It is Betsy who eventually speaks, informing him that so far nothing has been arranged. She is right. I haven't given my birthday any thought, and it seems that neither has my family, including Captain John.

As we walk home, my fingers tingle from Luke's touch, and my stomach feels strange. How did Luke know of my birthday? He must have asked someone about me, and that thought makes my insides quiver, in such an unfamiliar way. Betsy enquires as to what I would like to do for my birthday, but in truth, I care not a bit. Being nineteen will be the same as eighteen; I'll still be married to him.

August 14th 1853

It has been over a month since I lost the baby, yet so far my courses have not returned. I had considered my life changing for the better since reading Captain John's telegram a few days ago, but he returned early that evening, and continued in his black despair, or whatever ails him, by locking himself away in his study once more.

Hargreaves assures me that the brandy is near to finishing, and we expect that he'll be called to replenish at some point, but I refuse to allow Captain John's behaviour to affect the staff, and insist they go to their beds. It is some time in the early hours that I hear the smash of glass, and after wavering for a while, I hear Hargreaves in the hallway, and force myself out of bed.

A small group has congregated by the time I join them, as more sounds are heard erupting from the study. I send the maids, and cook back to their rooms, but bade Hargreaves to accompany me to investigate, of which he did without question, insisting he lead. Gratefully I do not argue, and together we descend downstairs.

On nearing the closed study door it becomes apparent to both of us that Captain John is the one creating the disturbances, and to rescue Hargreaves from any awkwardness I send him back to his own bed, with assurances that I will be fine. He retreats with reluctance, but I believe he understands my need for his discretion and departs with a bow.

The door is unlocked and I open it with
some trepidation, unsure what I will find.
I find my husband sitting amongst
broken glass, and over-turned furniture,
with his head in his hands, crying. He
does not hear me at first, and I fancy
that I can and shall retreat slowly, and
silently, but instead I find myself firmly
rooted to the spot. This was a side of my
husband I have never witnessed and I feel
compelled to watch, with some
fascination, but also a touch of
satisfaction at seeing Captain John
unhappy.
He turns and sees me then and his
appearance changes dramatically, in an
instant. Wiping the tears away, he
abruptly stands and straightens out his
clothing, all the while staring back at me,
daring me to say a word of what I have
witnessed. He then walks towards me, a
little unsteadily due to his consumption of
alcohol, stopping only inches from my
face.

He enquires as to the state of my body. I do not answer and he punches the wall behind me making me flinch with the impact. I lie and tell him my courses have returned. I hope my lie will keep me safe this night, but he leans closer to me and questions it. One hand reaches under my nightgown, and finds out my untruth. I am rewarded with a wicked smile, and there on the study floor among the glass and debris I am made to pay.

August 20th 1853

Since that night, Captain John continues his husbandly duties to produce an heir every day and night. My body is covered with bruises and I feel so unclean. But as quickly as Betsy is helping me scrub myself, and anoint my skin with lavender, he arrives home to apply more abuse to my body, and so it has been these last days. He says that he will impregnate me before he leaves for his barracks and then I will be expected to follow him, once he has procured a home suitable for an officer and his wife.

I am mortified. I expected to stay here
but it is not to be. There shall be no
respite for me until I produce an heir,
and even then it may never end.

This war is affecting everyone. I feel it in
the air, a tension that sits on every man's
face. Captain John refuses to indulge me
in any conversations regarding it. I think
he suspects my secret hopes that he will
go to Russia, and die. Such hopes are not
like me, but I cannot deny them any
longer.

My birthday yesterday was pitiful. He
gave me a pearl necklace, and I received
telegrams from Mother and Father,
wishing me a pleasant day. David also
sent a note of birthday wishes from all of
them, and that was my day. No party
with friends, no romantic dinner with a
man I love, nothing to celebrate my
ageing.

Dear Betsy, Mrs. Martins the cook and
Annabelle, surprised me with a small
gathering, with cake, sandwiches and tea
for luncheon, of which I was grateful and
near to tears at such kindness.

It was abruptly cut short on Captain John's return. He expected to give me another birthday present, one that I did not want, but had no choice in the matter. Excusing myself and thanking the ladies, I followed him to our bedroom. And so my birthday passed, and today I wish my husband dead.

August 23rd 1853

There truly is a God. My mother has unexpectedly arrived as she is visiting friends nearby. She never went to see her friend in Cheshire, due to Katherine's grief and their mourning of Andrew. Her manner towards me is fairly cold and distant, but I care not. My reward is reprieve from the assaults on my body and I smile warmly; we retire to my parlour.

Captain John attempts to keep his fury from showing and does it fairly well, but I am aware of his looks when Mother's attention is elsewhere, and I hope that Mother remains far longer than expected. She does. Deciding to stay over, she will visit her old friend on the morrow once she is refreshed. I rejoice in having her with me, and more so when Captain John takes his leave for another engagement with his regiment, assuring Mother that if he'd known of her arrival, he would have cancelled.

Mother and I dined and talked of Katherine who is healing slowly, though has shown no move to contact me. I pretend to feel indifferent as it is expected, but inside I am hurting. Mother informs me of a cousin who recently married and has produced a daughter, Primrose Caroline, which inevitably moves onto my own inadequate pregnancy.

I have no warning of my tears, but suddenly there they were. Mother believing that I am remorseful and grieving holds me close, and murmurs all the words I dread; that it will happen soon and that I am young. I can bear it no longer, and without conscious thought, the words come tumbling out. Of my unhappiness, and my brute of a husband, and my joy that I lost his child, and the abuse I suffer day and night by his hands.

I will forever remember the look on my mother's face. She went very pale, quickly taking sips from her wine glass. Taking a long deep breath, she bids me a good night and walks towards the door. I jump up and tear open my dress to reveal the bruises left by Captain John's hands, on my arms, my chest and neck, but she refuses to look.
"Look Mother, this is what you married me too …" I hope for an apology, a sincere look of remorse, of horror.

Instead, she stops at the doorway and says, "Get with child Margery, and your world will improve greatly. Do your duty, and I'm sure this will become unnecessary." I watch her walk upstairs. I can scarcely comprehend such indifference.
She left early this morning with barely a word.

August 27th 1853

Captain John has finally left. I rejoice quietly as I sup my early morning tea, and watch Betsy clear away thrown clothes from the floor. Last night I was assaulted again, but I have found a new potential action to annoy Captain John, I lie unmoving, and as always unresponsive. I lie as if dead, staring up at the ceiling, ignoring every attempt to gain my attention; it worked. Captain John climbed off me full of contempt and unfinished and stormed out of the bedroom, slamming the door behind him.

It is only then that I smile to myself and vigorously wipe my face to un-do the feel of that vile moustache against my skin, and remove his stinking breath. He doesn't return. I assume he has retired to his dressing room, where he sometimes collapses, too drunk to make it to his bedroom. I dream of the day he becomes too intoxicated and falls over the banister, to plunge to his death on the marble floor below. Wicked? I do not know, nor care on the matter. I would be rid of Captain John any way I can to be free.

He leaves while it is still dark outside. I hear him talking to Hargreaves; the poor man has to endure his master leaving at such an ungodly hour. He does not come to wake me, or say goodbye, and I am glad of it. His 'gifts' are cruel and unwelcome. His pearl necklace lies untouched in my jewellary box; I hate it, it chokes me. Perhaps that is why he bought it. I will not wear it unless ordered to.

I am expecting his parents to dine this evening, in what I presume is a need to comfort one another with Captain John's departure. I feel no need for comfort or company, but I will endure it regardless.

August 29th 1853

My courses are unquestionably late. I am pregnant again, I am sure of it. It has been two days since Captain John left. I am enjoying my newfound freedom to consider the matter, but today I vomit and feel the strange hardness that tells me my fate. I endured his parents the other night. They came with a few other acquaintances, and constantly glanced at me as though they expected news. They can wait. I am at least four weeks. Even as I count, I believe I already know the dreadful outcome and touch the area where his child grows. A mere dot so I'm told at such an early stage, but a dot of his nonetheless.

I walk the length and breadth of the park in hopes of exhausting myself and I will lose it. I run up and down my bedroom when alone, hoping my exertion may do something to dislodge it from my body. So far, to no avail.

I receive a telegram from Captain John informing me of his purchase of a dwelling fit enough for himself near his barracks, and my company is expected within the week. I tear it up and burn it. Today I ride in the carriage and head further into the countryside. We stop at a river and Betsy and I walk along it, admiring the pretty cottages and the variety of trees that litter the area. I know what I am doing. I am staying away from his house, so that I may not receive any more messages from him. I know it is futile, but I hate being there. I feel so constricted.

On our return, we dine in a pretty tea shop, talking about this and that, though in truth, I am aware of Betsy's scrutiny, and her need to voice her concerns for my overindulgences. I voice them for her, to save her any awkwardness, and inform her of my newest horror, and my necessity to keep moving before boredom, and this pregnancy takes hold. She understands both. We make our plans.

September 2nd 1853

Yesterday we took the carriage to the train station and boarded a train to the city of Chichester where we will embark on a two day adventure. We are staying in the old Blossoms hotel. An indulgence I will no doubt pay for with more than words, but to be frank, I believe that I have indeed earned this holiday. I call it a late birthday present to myself, and am determined to enjoy it immensely.

Betsy is more reserved of which I understand, but I refuse to consider the consequences. After all, I am carrying his child, what can Captain John do to me that he hasn't already?

I find the city beautiful and busy. The hotel is wonderful and I am being treated very well by the friendly staff. We must have walked for hours this morning. History interests me, so we have been looking for any remnants of the Roman occupation. We find very little sadly, besides bumps in the grass where Roman baths had once been. We visited the 12th century cathedral and a few of the smaller churches in the surrounding area, before retiring for lunch back at the hotel.

I feel exhausted and in need of a small lie down. So far the nausea that harmed me in the previous pregnancy has not come back as badly. Once I vomit, I feel fine and so must indulge in this one, ugly action every morning, and then my appetite returns with a passion. My limbs feel heavy and my feet swollen after so much exertion, but I insist on continuing our adventures. His child will not ruin my life. At times I feel older than my years, and a strange sorrow weighs on me.

By the early evening I feel well enough to dine in the restaurant with Betsy as my companion. She worries, but we have clothed her in one of my own dresses. She looks like any other lady. Besides, I do not wish to dine alone, and we enjoy a nice evening together, though we giggle rather frequently as we sip champagne, and Betsy is in turmoil at being found out. I think she enjoys the food; I find it delicious.

September 4th 1853

On our return to his home late in the afternoon, I am met by his parents who had been informed of my absence, and immediately came to investigate, assuming I had absconded for good. Oh what a scandal that would have been, and one I would gladly bear if it were not for my own family's honour at stake.

They are as always, cold and accusing. I am reproached for behaving like an ungrateful wife. They suggest that I am behaving in an abhorrent manner that brings shame to the family. They even attempt to accuse me of absconding with another man, to which I can remain silent no longer, and laugh out loud at such a ridiculous accusation.

My amusement is not met favourably, and it is deemed best that I retire to my room to rest. I remain where I am, which is met with more hostility and name calling. I remain seated throughout the duration and then quietly ask them to leave my house. I explain that as they are obviously stressed over such a trivial matter I deem it unnecessary for them to remain. They leave with black looks to find accommodation overnight, before returning home the next morning without any apology from me.

After my initial brazen behaviour, I now feel a cold dread come over me. Captain John can do whatever he chooses with me if pushed, regardless of a pregnancy or not. I have heard terrible stories of women who have been incarcerated by their families for being out-spoken. In their eyes, it is a justification to lock her up to promote milder behaviour. I could never endure such cruelty and yet, what have I endured so far these last months? I refuse to be submissive any longer. I have found weaknesses that I can use against him through my actions and deliberate deeds. I am determined to show Captain John that I will not obey him.

I am about to retire to bed when Hargreaves comes to find me, a telegram on the tray. I tell him to burn it.

September 5th 1853

This morning I receive another telegram demanding I remove myself from his home, and travel to the barracks where he will meet me off the train in two days time. I tear it up and throw it in the fire. I have no intention of going anywhere. A few hours later I receive yet another informing me that he is aware of my behaviour towards his parents and again demands that I depart for London on the train specified. I tear it up and throw it in the fire.

I may be behaving in an illogical manner, but instead I urge Betsy to pack my bags for another journey; I make plans to visit Katherine.

Although I have not heard from her and this hurts me greatly, I must face her and put right the terrible thoughts that are aimed against me. I must tell her that I suspect my husband of keeping any telegrams from me, and refused to allow me to attend little Andrews funeral, or comfort my own sister. It has been months now since his death, surely she can hold no grudge against her innocent sister?

I admit to feeling fearful and am not completely sure of my welcome, but this is my only chance of visiting Katherine and I must take it before this pregnancy holds me prisoner.

September 6th 1853

I am arrived at Katherine's home, and have retired to my room due to the sudden nausea caused by the long drive. I am also escaping the noise of the child that seems to fill every place in the house. Katherine behaves as though she cannot hear the squealing, or the crying of her daughter, Mary, who is nearly two. The nanny takes charge of little Mary for most of the time, but David and Katherine run a very informal home, and Mary is allowed to run wild.
I think that I cannot bear the racket of children, but Katherine smiles lovingly whenever Mary comes waddling into the room.

She allows her to climb onto her and fling her arms around Katherine's neck, thus putting an end to our conversation regarding her opinion of my behaviour. I have to leave at this point as watching such open acts of love makes me emotional, and I am not ready to share my horror with Katherine, certainly not after my mother's reaction. Katherine has heard my apology over the death of Andrew, but I do not inform her as to why I was hindered; that shall have to wait until we have more time alone. I am grateful that both she and David accept me into their home, even though both are a little off; I expected worse.

Betsy removes my dresses from the trunk and together we admire Annabelle's work. The green dress she made is exquisite, and I plan to show it off this evening before I get too big to wear it. Secretly I hope wearing a tight corset will remove his devil inside me before I show too much.

In truth, I have had long conversations with Betsy regarding childbirth, and know of its dangers and feel wholly against the idea of dying just to bring his spawn into the world. I feel nothing but revulsion at the idea of him having offspring. I know of nothing worse than to create a large family of Harrisons. His parents are particularly ghastly in their manners, and obviously failed appallingly in the upbringing of their sons. I am determined to believe that my own father would never tolerate such brutish behaviour from his own sons, had he been blessed with any.

Dinner this evening was thankfully a fairly quiet affair with only eight guests including myself. Considering I had barely given Katherine warning of my impending visit, so far she has behaved adequately towards me and has not referred to my appearance or of my husband's absence.

Annabelle's creation is admired, and I give her fully the recognition she deserves.

An elderly lady even enquires as to whether Annabelle would create a few dresses for her. I respond that I will indeed be obliged to allow Annabelle leave to fulfil such an honour as and when required.

Annabelle is such a young girl I envy her innocence and her ability to choose her own husband, if indeed there is ever a chance to encounter such a man. I must encourage her to grow her experiences and would hope these years spent with me will prepare her for a world where she can reach for whatever opportunities fall her way. If I can aid in these matters, then I shall endeavour to do so. I will try not to feel unjustly envious of the freedoms she has.

September 7th 1853

This morning Katherine finally approached me on the matter of my sudden visit. We are sitting in the garden watching her daughter with the nanny. We had just finished morning tea when she turned abruptly and I knew in that instant I am no longer welcome. Her words are spoken with some remorse, at least, I like to believe anyway, but the clear message is, that her husband is not comfortable with housing a wife who has clearly absconded from her husband in my condition. He has heard of Captain John's enquiries to various families, searching for his young wife and finds my actions quite distasteful. Katherine goes on to say, that although he loves me as a sister, he feels it is his duty to escort me back to my own home, and if necessary onwards to London considering my situation.

"And what are your thoughts on the matter?" I ask calmly, though in truth my insides are becoming very uncomfortable, and I have to stand to allow my body to stretch.

My sister at least has the decency to look ashamed when she tells me I should return to my husband, and be a good and loving wife, as that is my duty. I stare down at her then and she looks away, back to her child. I follow her gaze and admit it is a lovely picture of happiness and love, but then she has not married a monster.

I regret doing what I did next, but I am not thinking. I swiftly bend down close to Katherine and whisper everything I endure, before turning and walking away. I do not look back, nor do I thank my hosts for tolerating me. They are sending me into hell and I have nothing to thank them for as my escape routes narrow considerably. Betsy has my bags packed and we are back in the carriage within the hour. I do not believe that I shall see my sister again.

My return to Captain John's home this evening is met by downward glances, and mumbles by Hargreaves. The house has an air of death around it and I enquire as to the nature of it. Hargreaves merely shakes his head, before informing me that Captain John returned last night. My heart skips a beat and my stomach churns so badly I think I might faint. Betsy swiftly takes my cases upstairs, while Hargreaves carries the trunk. I turn towards the study to face my husband's wrath.

September 9th 1853

It has been two days since my return and still I am confined to my rooms. Betsy has been allowed to bring my food and help me dress, but Captain John remains nearby to deny any conversation between us. I see at once that Betsy has that same look of horror and pain on her face that I noticed later that evening when we arrived home. However I have not had a moment alone with her to enquire as to the nature of these mournful looks.

My encounters with Captain John have so far been minimal. On my return, he merely looked me up and down in disgust, informed me that we would be catching the Thursday train to London and I was required to remain in my rooms until such time. His disdain at my behaviour that he is required to leave his men, and take a leave of absence to find his wife is evident. My actions have brought shame on him. I do not care.

Something else is amiss, and it is this that haunts my thoughts. His lack of action has me feeling all the more afraid, as I am becoming more positive that something truly terrible has occurred in this house.

September 10th 1853

Thursday morning and I am already awake when Betsy comes in. I have barely slept since arriving home, my terror at leaving to go to another place causes me such fear that I cannot lie still, but walk the length and breadth of my room. His child continues to grow inside me and the area has become hard. I stare down where his devil resides and feel nothing but disgust at what is growing. I feel no love or compassion, only terror at what it will become if it lives.

I turn at the sound of the door opening and Betsy walks in to wake me for the journey ahead, and I see her unguarded face as she doesn't see me sitting at my dressing table in the semi-darkness.

"Tell me what has happened Betsy. This unknowing is driving me mad and do I not have enough horror's ahead of me that I cannot stand another?"

Betsy jumps on hearing my voice, spilling most of the cup of tea she is carrying, she sniffs loudly. She sets down the cup, turns and opens the curtains, revealing her bloodshot eyes and tearful cheeks. "I dare not. It is too evil to endure and you must focus on this trip and naught else."

"I cannot bear this journey as it is, and knowing something evil has occurred in my home, and I am to leave it behind, is truly unbearable to me. Please, I beg you Betsy, do not fail me now."

I almost got on my knees in that moment, and I said as much. I am so desperate to hear what horrors have so offended my staff. I feel compelled to add. "Do not have a care for this child, if it dies it is of no consequence to me, if the shock of hearing is too great."

Betsy hid her shock well, though in truth, she already knew of my contempt for Captain John's offspring.

It was then I heard in low whispers the true awfulness of what had occurred the night before my arrival home. I must confess that I swooned and needed reviving, and I did retch as each dreadful word passed Betsy's lips, but I had to know and now I knew the full extent of Captain John's evilness.

No one knows the true reason for his descent into the kitchens that night, most likely looking for more brandy, but he found Annabelle alone, sewing a dress as a surprise for my return. I was not available for him to unleash his fury at my transparent rebellion against him, and so he saw Annabelle as the next best thing. He defiled her innocent body, leaving her battered and bruised on the cold kitchen floor, warning her that she would be dismissed without references if she told anyone. He would sully her good name. A whore she would be known and nobody would believe her.

It was luck that Mrs Martins went to the kitchen to fetch some water hours later, and found her shivering and in shock. She helped her to her room that she shares with Betsy, cleaning her up, and put her to bed before we arrived home. Betsy was told almost immediately, and has since cared for the girl, who hasn't spoken a word, since telling Mrs Martins, but none is needed; they all know who is to blame for such a monstrosity.

I remain un-moving as Betsy informs me of how abominable my husband can behave. I feel sick and did indeed vomit again, and feel light-headed. Betsy helps me to the bed. I have to see her, to make amends, though I have no notion how I can do that. I can never return her purity; he has stolen it without remorse. Surely I, a lady can inform the authorities on her behalf? Would that not help her situation in some way or would my being his wife hold some difficulties? My head swims with possibilities and then he appears at the doorway, demanding to know why I am not dressed.

Only Betsy's warning touch on my arm stops me from telling him I know of his vile act on an innocent, though I believe my face gives it away. He merely looks me over and orders that I be ready in haste and then he leaves, leaving me in turmoil for Annabelle and my own situation. Justice has to prevail, yet I know no answer to reach its conclusion.

September 15th 1853

It has been days since we left his house in Horsham and arrived at the house in London near to the barracks. During our journey, we did not speak at all and have barely passed a sentence since arriving, as the horror of what my husband is capable of sinks in. I do not know why I told him of the new pregnancy, but I did, and I quickly told him how much I wished it dead. He stared at me with so much hatred, I felt a moment of terror, before he merely bowed his head, and continued to eat breakfast. I had no appetite.

The house is smaller than Horsham, with only four bedrooms, though the dining room and sitting room appear to be the same size. I have no parlour of my own, so have taken to spending time in the bedroom allocated to me. He has taken his own bedroom opposite mine on the understanding that he may visit at any time he wishes. My bedroom overlooks a small garden at the back of the house, enclosed by a high brick wall.

Apparently it is perfectly normal to have his family nearby. Though Horsham is a fairly short train and carriage ride, he prefers, like many other officers, to bring their families closer until they leave for the war. I am introduced to six other wives, and various offspring, and find nothing in common with any of them. Most are older than me by a few years, and look upon me as a young trouble-maker. It seems my reputation as a fleeing wife has reached all ears, and they watch me with both fascination and dislike.

I am also different, in that the wives seem to love their husbands, or they are far greater actresses than I give them credit for. I continue to despise mine. On our first night, he did indeed come to my room and demand that I make myself available to him pregnant or not. I refused, calling him all the names I can think of, though never actually revealing that I know of his act towards sweet, innocent Annabelle. He lunges towards me, grabbing my arm and pushes me onto the bed where he uses me for his own gratification before leaving me bloodied and in pain.

I have fought long and hard on the matter of Annabelle. Every ounce of my being wishes to report him to the authorities, however, having spoken with Betsy, she advised me against it, for Annabelle's sake. The chances of being taken seriously were minimal, and Annabelle would lose her position and an income. It is unfair and cruel, but for now, I am helpless against the system judged by men.

September 17th 1853

I am informed that war has broken out,
and that his regiment will be dispatched
to fight. He came to tell me himself.
"I can assure you Madam that I shall
return and you will continue to be mine."
"Then I sincerely hope with all my heart
that a bullet finds you before you dare to
return. You are a monster, unworthy of
me and this innocent child I carry. I wish
you rot in hell for your crimes." is my
reply.
Captain John grins wickedly. "I will enjoy
making you suffer for that remark
Madam. Knowing your hatred of me
only spurs me on to commit these acts
you find so repulsive. It is my right to
have you woman. I own you."
It is only after he leaves the room that I
realise my words. 'An innocent child', I'd
said. Did I mean such words? I certainly
did hope he died. Regardless, my dream
has come true. If God is listening, he could
get killed and the devil can take his own.

I have prayed every day to be released of him. The day has finally come. He returns briefly to inform me that his parents will be arriving to take care of me in my pregnancy. I smile at this news. Captain John is going to war, he might die. He doesn't trust me to care for his heir so he sent for his parents. Was he right to do so?

It seems all of it is happening quicker than expected. Captain John has two days to prepare his regiment and receive orders and supplies. The decision to give aid has been given; now, they must act and do so quickly. The journey will take weeks, and so suddenly, there is an air of urgency everywhere you look. The wives are upset and frightened. The men are excitable and sure of themselves and victory. I remain aloof, quiet and count the days.

September 20th 1853

There were no fond farewells. No kisses goodbye. I don't even watch him go. I show my contempt for him by my absence. I can hear the cheers, and the applause for the regiments, as they march out of the barracks. I feign sickness as my excuse not to watch him leave. Nobody believes me.
Four hours later, his parents arrive. His mother cries openly regarding his going to war, I do nothing but yawn at such tedious actions for a monster. She calls me cold and heartless. "And your opinion of me is irrelevant." I answer. Followed by, "Your appearance at this house is not welcome, and you may take your leave whenever it pleases you if I am so cold and heartless. Perhaps you should look towards your own behaviour which has concluded in your son's abhorrent actions." I abruptly depart the room, leaving them both open mouthed, and staring at such an outrage.

September 23rd 1853

Breakfast is a silent affair, as is lunch and dinner. I am confined to the house and garden on Captain John's orders, due to my losing the last heir. Hargreaves who has travelled up after closing the Horsham house, is thankfully willing to help me in any escapes. Today, the third day after their arrival, he informs them that I have retired to my rooms as I am feeling tired. In truth, he sneaks me down through the kitchens, out into the back garden and through a side gate that leads onto a narrow alley where a carriage waits. With Betsy accompanying me, we head into town to explore, and buy some necessaries. It is a most pleasant afternoon. Made all the more so as they never had a clue.

September 29th 1853

These small deceptions become a regular event. The household, who see how I am treated, have taken my side, and aid in my escapes to either London, a park, or I walk along the river. Yesterday I had the privilege of visiting a museum and an old church, all without his mother or father in tow. I believe Hargreaves is educating the new staff in the behaviour of Captain John, and therefore the women especially, are forthcoming in their aid. The groom, gardener and Hargreaves, are all content in helping a lady in distress, as they are gentlemen, so much more so than my husband.

We dine in silence for the most part, though Gloria will note something amiss, whether it is my attire or the house is not clean enough. George barely glances my way, beyond a quick checking of my waistline with a satisfied nod. I feel like a filly that holds the grand sire of someone important.

I pity the child in a way. So much rests on this little one's shoulders. God help it if it is a girl. I cannot be more than six or seven weeks into this pregnancy and yet, it feels so much longer. The sickness continues each morning, and disappears once I have forced some food down. Each thing I endure is another reminder of him.

We receive a telegram that his regiment is safe and marching forward with honour. Sir George informed me at dinner this evening.

"Are you not pleased my dear? Your husband is fighting with honour."

I shrug and say nothing. Gloria calls me something derogatory, before Sir George quietens her. I'm not listening and excuse myself from the table. I cannot help but wonder at their reaction should they know what men their sons have become. What is it that makes such men find pleasure in wickedness? I have watched Sir George and can see nothing in his demeanour that would convince me of his own cruelty. Gloria never flinches from him or glares with revulsion. I believe their marriage to be one of mutual respect, if not love.

October 2nd 1853

Sir George, my father-in-law has been rather scarce lately, thankfully. He has taken to going out. God only knows where to help pass the day. I have a suspicion that he is in one of those awful men's clubs, where women are banned so men can continue to believe that they rule the earth. However, his leaving means that Gloria is with me almost constantly these last few days, and so my own escapes have had to stop for a while; my nerves are rather frayed already.

My trips out consist of short carriage rides in the country, with Gloria. Short walks in a nearby park, with Gloria and visiting other wives whose husbands are also away in the Crimean war. We drink tea and eat small sandwiches whilst the wives hark on about how lonely they are, and how worried, while Gloria enjoys holding court, as one whose son has gone to a war so far away to do his duty. Anyone would think Captain John is fighting the Russians bare-handed and alone, the way she carries on.

I merely smile and nod in all the right places, but deflect any comments regarding my concerns for Captain John, for I have none. He can die an agonising death for all I care, so can his parents and his brother. All I require is to be left in peace, and that includes being rid of this growing burden that refuses to die. I am not sure if I mean these words for the growing child. I feel varying emotions towards it.

When I am alone at night and can finally allow my mind to unravel, my thoughts stray to darling Annabelle. Is she healing in both body and mind? I have requested Betsy send a telegram to Mrs Martins, the cook, to enquire, but so far we have received nothing in return and Hargreaves informs me that neither of my in-laws have intercepted any mail. I can only pray that she is healing, and that Captain John pays for his crime one way or another. Hargreaves is not saying anything regarding his niece's condition. I fantasise that he takes his revenge on Captain John in some dreadful manner. Surely he is within his right to do such a thing.

October 4th 1853

Last night our sleep is interrupted by a loud knocking on the front door. Hargreaves and George went to investigate and found a woman on the step holding a small infant. She begged to speak with Captain John but on being told that he had departed to fight, she wept hysterically. To hinder any gossip, she was compelled to enter and explain herself. At this moment I had risen and stood at the top of the stairs to listen. It is plain to anyone looking that the young woman is a lady of little virtue. Her dress reveals rather too much for decency, but it is her air of the street that gives her away instantly. She speaks well, and one can imagine her coming from a respectable family who perhaps has fallen on hard times, and having no choice has given herself to men. She asks for a drink but is denied, until I force myself to move from my hiding place and make myself visible.

Much to Sir George's annoyance I continue to ignore his ranting that she must be removed. Instead I indicate the sitting room and she goes in, a look of gratitude passing her eyes, and one of defiance on catching a glare from George. I ignore him completely, making it clear this is my home and that he can return to his bed. He did thus, with a grunt. Thankfully the fire is still embers, so the room has some warmth to it. I indicate the drinks cabinet, but the woman does not move towards it but rather lays her sleeping infant on the nearest chair and sits down next to it.

"I'd meant a warm drink as I'm frozen through, but if you'll oblige me Missus, I'll take a small nip as it helps keep the babe warm and sleeping."

I have no notion as to what she means, but again offer her my hospitality, and wait with bated breath as she pours herself a small whiskey and returns to the chair.

"Who are you?"

On my enquiry she actually blushes and looks ashamed. As her words flow, I realise why and on calculations I remember how months earlier Captain John behaved in a strange way, locking himself in his study and disappearing all night. He'd looked like a man haunted and disturbed; now I saw why. He had fathered a boy, an heir when I had lost one, but it was a boy he could never acknowledge as his own. Apparently it distressed him to a large extent because he had fallen for this lady who introduces herself as Margaret, or Maggie as she is known.

Margaret goes on to tell me how she and Captain John had met in an ale-house night after night, and she fell in love with him as much as he for her. I had been correct in my first assumption. Margaret did come from a decent and God-fearing family up in Lancashire. A merchant who had done well for himself and his family had moved up in the world, only to lose it all through lost cargo at sea.

Margaret's mother died of starvation, refusing to eat while her little ones needed feeding. Margaret, being the oldest girl of three and a toddling boy had watched the women near the docks earning regular money, and hadn't thought it very hard. I beg her not to continue and she falls silent, sipping her whiskey as I scrutinise her and the babe. It came to pass that Captain John left her, weeks before the birth, with a little money and then disappeared. It has taken these months to trace his whereabouts. She has travelled from Sussex hoping to receive assistance, as the few pennies he'd left her with have long since gone, and she fears for her child.

Without hesitation I invite her to collect her child and follow me. This she does without question, though I see a flicker of anxiety in her eyes. I know she expects to be turned out, but I am no such fiend as Captain John, or his parents.

Using a candle to light our way, I walk into the fairly warm kitchen and find some biscuits, milk and bread. Handing them to Margaret I lead the way into a tiny room used for storing bits and pieces. It has a couple of horse blankets folded up in the corner. I lie these out on the hard floor and go further down the hall to a room used for the laundry and return with some blankets. I bade her make her and the child as comfortable as possible and I would continue our conversation in the morning.

October 5th 1853

I have seen my 'guest' again this morning, much to Sir George and Gloria's loathing. Gloria is refusing to leave her rooms until that 'harlot' is removed from the house. For this I would keep Margaret here indefinitely if it would allow me some peace from my mother-in-law.

Sir George is willing to hear her tale, though having spoken with him this morning I can see no reprieve for Margaret in their eyes. He has already condemned her as a liar, and a whore. One of which may be true, however, I am willing to hear her story, and shall hold my judgment until she is finished.

We retire to the sitting room sipping tea whilst we listen to Margaret's story. Although I heard it last night, I admit that my mind hasn't taken it all in. Even my sleepless night mulling her words over and over have not aided in my conclusion of how to approach this latest horror of Captain John's behaviour.

I cannot deny that I believe her story. The circumstances and Captain John's behaviour, all fit perfectly around the time of the babe's age. I knew back then that something was amiss, now here before me sits the evidence of it. The child lies asleep in his mother's arms. Once she has finished her story to Sir George, I immediately stand and take the child in my own arms. Not from affection, but on seeing how thirsty, and hungry, the mother is from regaling us with her tale.

My gaze shifts to Sir George who hasn't spoken but is standing staring out of the large windows overlooking the meadow beyond. We women exchange glances and Margaret sips her tea. I hold my husband's disloyalty. I will admit that in that long silence, I feel a strange stirring inside towards the sleeping child. Its eyelashes resting gently on pink cheeks, a little too lean for my liking, his rose-bud mouth, small and tiny. In my understanding, children's cheeks should be bonny and plump, and a sparkle to the eyes. Even through the thin material and blanket I can feel ribs, and the babe weighs almost nothing.

"What is it?"

Sir George's voice cuts through my mental examination of the child, and I look up to find him staring at me. It is Margaret who answers him.

"A boy. I've named him Jonathan James, after his father."

"His father? How can you be so sure this illegitimate boy comes from my stock? As I see it, you're a whore, who opens her legs to any poor soul. Did you see my son in an ale-house, and think to use his good name to reach higher status? Think again, girl!"

Turning to me Sir George bows slightly. "Forgive my language Margery. I am outraged at this woman's behaviour."

I remain speechless.

Margaret remains sitting following this tirade, but eventually she stands, replaces her empty tea cup, and takes the child from my arms. Turning to Sir George she thrusts the child in front of his face. "A whore I may be, but if you do not know your own grandson, who I'll swear, is the image of his father, Captain John, James Harrison, then to hell with you sir! I have been badly used by your son who promised me I'd be cared for. He wept in my arms knowing he could not acknowledge his child that he so greatly desired. He swore to remain by my side, but fled three weeks before his son was born."

Sir George shook his head. "I do not believe woman that my son would stay with you, when married to a respectable young woman, who carries his legitimate child. You lie!"

Turning to me she looked abashed.

"Forgive me my lady, you have been nothing but kindness towards me, in what can only be described as an awful situation. I have done you wrong madam, and I sincerely apologise."

"Fine words indeed, but what proof I say, do you have that this boy is my son's?"

Margaret turned to Sir George and again held out the child. "Look with your eyes sir, and if that is not enough, then send word to Captain John that I am here, and require his word, on his honour."

Sir George laughed a cruel laugh, "My son is fighting a war, harlot. What madness would induce me to send any message on such a trivial matter as this that is so obvious a ploy, to entice money from my son?"

"I will send a telegram to his regiment. Perhaps he will receive it, perhaps not, but we owe it to this child to attempt such a message, and also to Captain John to redeem his honour."

The words were out of my mouth before I considered them, but once they are, I know them to be the right course of action, regardless of Sir George's objections. To further his outrage I ask Margaret to remain in the house, until such time as our predicament can be cleared one way or another. Much to my humour, both he and Gloria leave within the hour, and I can claim some semblance of peace in my own home.

October 7th 1853

Days pass in a blur. Margaret and her son have been allocated a small attic room next to the maid's bedroom. I insist that she claim the room, and make it as comfortable as possible, though in truth it has a bad draft and no fire. More blankets are found, and clean, respectable clothing, found for both her and the child.

Every morning we wait with bated breath for the post, but so far we have received no word from Captain John, neither have I heard from my in-laws. I did receive a brief letter this morning from my mother enquiring if the rumours were true regarding a certain type of lady staying with me. No mention of the child of which I found to be most interesting. My in-laws will spread rumours of a harlot staying, but never word of an illegitimate grandson. Hypocrites indeed!

Margaret hovers in the corners of the house, trying desperately to be invisible. I hear her attempting to keep her son quiet, and have sought her out to reassure her he is not a problem to me. Yesterday evening, I believe she finally relaxed enough to feel a trifle more comfortable to speak with me. She spoke with no one else, and none of my staff will indulge in conversation anyway knowing her occupation. I have attempted to assure them all that Margaret is a wronged woman. They believe they are being loyal to me. I sincerely appreciate that.

As I say, yesterday she found me staring outside. I'd recently felt a small shift moving deep inside me and I was waiting for the nausea to abate. Having Margaret around and seeing her son has stirred something within me, and I am trying to fight against it. I did not, no, that is not the truth of it, I CANNOT feel anything for Captain John's offspring. The devil can only spawn the worst kind of being and yet, looking at Margaret's son, I can't see, nor feel anything untoward. He is a babe, an innocent and it causes me such confusion as to how I feel about the child growing in my own belly.

"Do you hate him?" she asks me. I jump at the sound of her voice having not heard her enter.

I hesitate before answering, unsure if it is proper to be so informal with this woman, but honesty wins. "Yes. I hate him."

She doesn't seem shocked by my unconcealed hatred of my husband. In fact, she smiles, and moves to sit by the fire.

"Because he was forced onto you?" Margaret settles the baby more comfortably in her arms and waits for my answer.

"Yes, though his cruelty does nothing to abate my hatred of him. He has done nothing to aid in my comfort, nor has he shown me affection. I am merely a thing to own, and do with whatever he fancies, at any time he chooses. I am not his wife, I am his property." I spat out the last sentence and abruptly sit as the wave of venom comes over me. I have never voiced such truth before, and never to a whore. It feels wonderful and cleansing, and I smile. Margaret smiles back.

"I understand my lady. Captain John is not an easy man to love, but may I say that he also felt obliged to the match. So far as I'm told, his father sought you out, and having approved of you, he insisted his son marry you to align both houses. John felt obliged to his father and after knowing you for some time, he found you pleasing."

I am astonished by this declaration and say as much. I am unsure what to think, or feel, on hearing that Captain John had been as reluctant to marry me, as I was to be wed. However, I cannot forget Annabelle, and my loathing of him.
I am considering informing Margaret of the kind of man she allowed herself to fall for, when the door opens and Hargreaves enters with a telegram. With shaking hands I open it. Captain John has been wounded, a head injury. He is being confined to the officer's hospital, and enclosed was the telegram we had sent, informing him of his child. I feel nothing except disappointment. Captain John lives.

October 11th 1853

After informing my in-laws of their son's injuries, though I knew very little, I hear nothing back from them. I consider this extremely rude, though not surprising.

I hear that Sir George is considering the journey, though it could take many weeks now as autumn sets in, and it is a cold one. We hear that snow has begun to fall in Scotland and feel the icy breath of an early winter. I slipped yesterday on some wet leaves on one of my brief strolls around the garden and I wait to see if any blood will come - so far, nothing. It seems this babe is stronger than I care for.

I hoped to do a little shopping, but now that I have slipped, nobody is allowing me outside. Besides a slight ache in my ankle, I feel fine. My family keep in touch briefly, but I receive no invites to dine from anyone, and I feel as though I have the plague. I remember dancing and laughing and feeling happy once, so long ago. I look in my mirror and see a stranger looking back at me, and I despise her.

Margaret is my only companion. Betsy's opinion is unchanging of her, and has taken to leaving the room when Margaret appears. But I persevere in my attitude. I cannot see Margaret as the whore, the lowly woman who stole my husband. I see the love she bears for him, and although I cannot fathom how it is, I also cannot argue that she feels it, and so who am I to judge her? This man was forced onto me; Margaret chose him, and is willing to have his son. I cannot condemn her for this unselfish act.

October 15th 1853

I receive a telegram that Sir George has begun his journey to see for himself the full extent of his son's injuries. Richard has gone with him. They left this morning for France and it is hoped that Captain John will be transferred to a hospital half way between Gallipoli and Paris. The full extent of his head injuries are still not known, but Sir George hopes that this last week has given him time to heal enough to be moved.

And so, it seems that my life will not be improving, as my husband has not had the decency to die in a damned war, where thousands are dying. No, he merely receives a head injury in the first encounter with the enemy, making him incapacitated, but alive. I truly believe God hates me for some past indiscretion, or perhaps in another life, I was truly evil.

Of course I never divulge the full extent of my feelings on the matter, though I believe Margaret suspects. Our days are shared in companionship, strange as that may seem. Having heard Captain John is alive, though to what extent is yet to be seen, I fear that I cannot ask her to leave, and the truth of it is, I don't want her to. I have come to enjoy our talks. Margaret is plain speaking, and forthright, which is wonderful. Betsy is keeping her opinions to herself, but I can guess her thoughts. Whenever I broach the subject of Margaret and the child, Betsy purses her lips, narrows her eyes, and mumbles something incoherent. I must admit to finding this amusing, but keep that to myself.

I have no notion as to what the gossip is regarding Margaret's presence in my home, but I am not foolish enough to think that word has not reached all of the county, of such a scandalous situation. I care not a jot! It is refreshing to not have to put on airs and graces for the upper classes. Besides my occasional nausea, and my growing belly, I am fairly well. Life is grand without my monster of a husband here to abuse my body. I feel melancholy on occasion, and miss the parties, and the social engagements with other women, but mostly, I am content in my bubble.

Do not think me naive. If Captain John dies, as his widow I will receive something of his estate, though I have no idea if he has made a will, or indeed mentioned me within it, but my situation will be anxious, to be sure, especially if this child lives. On hindsight, if Captain John's spawn lives, then my situation may actually flourish, as I shall have a bargaining tool with the Harrisons; something positive to consider at least. So that is two encouraging things that may occur if my husband dies.

A third enters my head - Luke Babbleton.
I think of him often, though he gives me
no cause to consider him in any other
way than a friend, well, perhaps more of
an acquaintance, but I believe that if
Captain John does die, then he may
proceed further. Mere wishes on my part
I'm sure, but a dream I hold onto
nonetheless.

October 17th 1854

Today I enquire about Annabelle again,
and insist on being told the whole horrific
tale. My cook at first insists that she
knows nothing, but on Hargreaves
returning from another errand, he hears
the backend of the conversation and
knows that I ask out of real concern.
Hargreaves kindly tells me of his niece.

Annabelle has recovered physically from her ordeal but is struggling mentally. Mrs Martins, the cook at our Horsham house, is taking good care of her, and I am grateful to her. Thankfully no child has been forced upon her young body, but she can neither eat nor sleep from the nervous tension, and is quickly wasting away. Nobody and nothing can bring her comfort, her sorrow is too deep.

I weep on hearing the words spoken with such abhorrence. Mrs Martins made it perfectly clear that she blames me in some way for the poor girl's misery, and I do not question it. Hargreaves is reluctant to tell me this information, but I urge him. He confesses that he also felt a grievance against me, but realises his mistake and apologises. I beg him not to. Mrs. Martins sat in silence, listening to our conversation. She wipes her eyes with the back of her apron.

"I admit my lady, I did indeed believe that you knew of this deed and had remained silent for all the wrong reasons. Now, I admit, that having seen, and heard what I have, I do not hold you responsible in any way for this crime.

For have you not suffered, as this poor child does? And do you not continue to do so?"

It takes me a few moments to compose myself to answer her as I feel overwhelmed by her sincerity. I thank her for her honesty, to which she breaks down and asks for forgiveness. I give it willingly and she abruptly gets up to prepare some tea. I am glad of it, as I have considered my household my friends of a sort, and I would hate for it to have been false. In that moment, I have such a strong urge to hug the woman, I do not know what to do, so quickly instruct Hargreaves to fetch Betsy; I am going home, back to Horsham regardless of Captain John's orders. I have to see for myself the ruin of Annabelle, and hopefully save her life even if my husband has destroyed it.

October 19th 1854

I am writing this as we stop on our way home due to both my fatigue and Margaret's child becoming too agitated by the bouncing around of the carriage. I decided to bring Margaret with me, as her presence in the London home may have been too unpleasant for the staff to contemplate. Margaret readily agrees, though I tell her nothing of my reasons. It seems I have a friend who is willing to comfort me on such a long trip. Betsy remains silent. I miss our long talks, but she has become subdued, and broody, since Margaret's arrival, and has already spoken of her contempt at such a low standing woman living in my home.

I care not a fig of Margaret's old occupation, in fact; I find some of her stories to be entertaining, if a trifle vulgar in places. Yet one cannot expect to hear stories from a whore, and find them to be as clean as a nun on Sunday. The travelling has been made to pass much quicker whilst she regales me with her adventures.

She sleeps now in the room next door that I acquire for herself, the babe and Betsy, much to her horror. Hargreaves assures me he will remain with the carriage and sleep in the barn. The inn we are resting in is fairly busy, and judging from the sounds downstairs there is much jolly going on. Having secured my door, I stand for a long time listening to the singing and merry-making, and wonder if Margaret feels the pull of the familiar sounds, as a prostitute must know. Temptation fills my soul for a moment, and I fiddle with the latch. What would happen were I to wander downstairs without a chaperone? I go to my bed pondering these thoughts and fall asleep to the sounds of singing.

October 20th 1853

We arrive tired and fretful today, and I am glad to see Hargreaves take control of everything. The house has continued to run with minimal staff and now as I rest in my room, I hear shouts and scurrying about as the house comes to life with people and purpose. I am ashamed to say that now I am arrived, finding Annabelle has become a responsibility I dread. Will my presence horrify the poor girl? Does she wish me ill will? I can neither blame her for such thoughts, nor condemn her for them. I feel the same misery, and sought refuge in my rooms for a time, to attempt to gather my thoughts.

The evening meal is an uncomfortable affair as nobody is particularly hungry, except for John James. His howling is abruptly silenced as Margaret takes herself away for privacy to feed her child. I am intrigued, and I almost ask her to stay, so that I may witness the feeding, but my manners refuse to allow such an idea, and I clamp my lips shut. I force down cold meat and potatoes, aware that the household is on bated breath, waiting for the 'confrontation' between myself and Annabelle. It is made aware to me by Margaret, that some consider Annabelle is to blame somehow, which appals me greatly, and I ask for her to be brought to my sitting room immediately.

I am sorry I have attempted to eat, as the food sits like rocks in my stomach, and my back aches terribly from the journey. I stand up and pace in front of the fire, willing this moment to end. Eventually a slight knock is heard and Annabelle enters, at least I think it is her. All life has left the girl. A mere shell walks timidly into the room, head bowed, tears evidently wiped away only seconds before. It occurs to me that she expects to be dismissed, and I move to her quickly, all nausea leaving me as I hold her tightly.

Her shock dissolves into sobs that rack her tiny frame. I hold on and let her cry. I know this will be frowned upon by my own class, but damn the lot of them. I have to pick up the pieces of my husband's evil act upon this girl, and if Annabelle wants to take it to the Metropolitan police, I will support her. It has crossed my mind on many occasions, but I'd been assured that it would most likely go against Annabelle. I've been appalled by such a revelation.

I am learning fast, just how man controls women, and have no doubt Annabelle would be discriminated against, purely because of her status in life. Her word against Captain John's would never win, especially without witnesses.

Once cried out, I walk Annabelle to the couch near the fire and eventually she stops shaking. Handing her one of my handkerchiefs, I wait while she composes herself as well as can be expected.

"Annabelle, I do not blame you in any way for this act against you by my husband. You must believe me on this."

I see some release of tension in her shoulders on hearing my words, and she finally looks up at me. My heart breaks to see such pain and sorrow.

"Let me reassure you dear, that I will support you in whatever path you wish to choose. Be it the police, or silence, or whatever else you desire, you have my full support. I cannot express my shame and horror at what Captain John has done to you. An apology seems so minimal in these circumstances, but you have my deepest regret. How can I help you?"

I wait patiently while Annabelle gathers her thoughts. It takes a long time for her to find the courage to speak, and when she does it is nothing more than a whisper.

"I ... I wish to leave your employ, and move far away, but I have nothing to support me ... My aunt lives in Scotland, and I considered going there ... but ..."

I sit back. It is inevitable to lose such a lovely and talented young lady after her ordeal, and yet it still comes as a shock.

"What does your aunt do?"

"She works as a ladies' maid, like Betsy, but she's talked of opening a ladies clothes shop in Edinburgh ..."

And there it is, a perfect opportunity for Annabelle. Her designs and dress-making are a talent indeed and I say as much.

"Then to your aunt you must go, and all expenses shall be met by me. My husband can compensate you. Nothing can repair what he did. I hope his money will help restore your life into a happier one."

October 24nd 1853

October 24nd 1853

Over the last couple of days, I sent
Hargreaves to various places around
Horsham to sell off Captain John's
belongings. A silver flask, some silver
goblets he treasures, along with boots and
jackets for a mere pittance. I also
entertain a gentleman who specialises in
portraits one afternoon, and sell him two
of Captain John's favourite scenes of a fox
hunt, that always sickened me.
 I've accumulated almost two hundred
pounds, including Captain John's
emergency money he keeps hidden
beneath a loose floorboard in his
bathroom. I found it by accident, well, to
be truthful, it was Betsy who noticed the
floorboard. That added another twenty
pounds. I feel utterly right in this course
of action, though I would much prefer to
see him hang for his crime. As it is, he has
done himself a favour by being injured in
his service to the crown, and will be
considered a hero. He is no such thing.
Captain John will never be anything
other than a monster.

October 25th 1853

Today Annabelle leaves. Her train
journey will be long and arduous but for
the first time I see a slight tinge to her
cheeks; she is free and away from the
scene of her ruin. I envy her. Younger
than me, she has endured hell and is now
free to live her life. I am stuck here, and I
cannot help but wish I am going with her.
That thought did occur to me as I bought
her tickets, but the truth is, I'd be found
and so would she. Like this, Annabelle
can disappear and begin to heal. I am a
constant reminder of her ordeal. Besides,
this is her journey of discovery, not mine.
Her compensation is in the bank and she
has ten pounds of my own money thrust
into her purse. It is all I can do for her
and I feel sorry for it.
I insist on Hargreaves taking her to the
station. I will not accompany her and
Annabelle agrees. "It is not because I am
your mistress and it would not be proper,
it is because I will cry on seeing you
leave. I will miss you Annabelle."

We did cry then, mistress and maid. No class, no barriers, but two women hurting by the same evil man. I press another handkerchief onto her and bid her farewell. I do not expect to hear from her again. Though I hope Hargreaves will keep me informed of her progress.

October 28th 1853

Three days have gone by since Annabelle's departure and I receive a telegram from my in-laws enquiring after my health (meaning, they are enquiring about his devil inside me) and am I agreeable to a visit, now that I have returned to Captain John's house without asking permission. It seems Sir George has returned from the hospital empty-handed, and they feel obliged to fill me in on whatever he found there.

Astonishingly, they arrive behaving in a
most pleasant manner. I am not blind to
the fact that Gloria repeatedly asks about
my health and the child's growth. They
are being polite and courteous due to my
pregnancy. It was around this time that I
lost the last one, and they don't want a
repeat of that disaster. No, they are here
to check up on their heir and make sure
Mummy is behaving herself. Nobody
mentions Margaret, who removes herself
to her attic room on their arrival.
The evening meal is delicious. My
appetite has returned on knowing
Annabelle is safely away and Captain
John has paid for it. Sir George, I notice,
glances at the empty wall, but says
nothing to me with regards to the two
paintings. Once the meal is over, we
retire to the sitting room and sit by the
fire. I wait.

With a brief glance at Gloria, Sir George begins. It seems Captain John has been injured in the head, and has a nasty wound on his leg, that is causing him excruciating pain. Sir George and Richard remained with him for a time and once they knew his leg could be saved, they relaxed a little. His head wound is now causing concern, in that he has memory lapses. One day he'll recognise his father, the next he doesn't. Gloria became upset at this point, but I ignore her. I am fighting the urge to smile. Captain John is in agony; Annabelle should hear this news.

Sir George has left him at the hospital to return home to pressing matters, leaving Richard with his brother, but he intends to return in the next day or so, to bring Captain John home. So far he is using a wheelchair but has been assured that it is only temporary, and he will be up and about in no time.

Their obvious concern is their heir, which means they are concerned for my well being and how this news might affect me. They do not wish to cause me any stress and want to reassure me that John will be able in a few months; they are sure of it. So it is put to me that when Captain John returns, that he remains with them, where he will be cared for, until such time as he recovers. I agree willingly and they leave satisfied.

I sit for a long time after their departure considering how it might be living with a monster who may not remember his past deeds. How will Margaret feel showing their child to a man who may in all probability, not recognise her? She loves him. I can never understand that, but she does and I refuse to condemn it.

November 5th 1853

It has been days since I last wrote. I must confess that I have been in a state of anxiety for the majority of the time due to hearing that Captain John is due home today if the travelling has gone according to plan. He will remain with his parents, a mere half a day's ride. It will be no concern of theirs to bring him here for a visit, to see if he remembers me, his child or his house. So far, I have received no word, and it is this that causes me constant worry.

All day I am searching outside for any sign of a telegram or their carriage. I cannot be still for long, and find myself pacing the house. This action angers me greatly. Have I not suffered enough, that although he is not here Captain John is still inflicting such torment at my door? By the time I go to bed, I am exhausted – no news from his parents.

November 6ᵗʰ 1853

Margaret insists we go out today. A walk in the park will do us both good. It has not passed me by that Margaret has also been anxious and unable to sit still for days. John James has also behaved as though disturbed. Perhaps he is feeling his mother's apprehension? I cannot fathom how she must feel regarding his parents' insistence that her child is not of their bloodline, and worse still, if the man she loves will never know her, will she therefore be doomed to live on the streets as a whore. I cannot allow that to happen to my new friend.

Our walk brings more than a welcome outing. It allows us to breathe and to talk freely, more so than indoors, where Margaret attempts to keep her presence to a minimum, for the sake of my staff, and for my own reputation as a lady. It has not gone un-noticed that visitors have disappeared these last few weeks and I am under no illusion as to the reason.

Having a prostitute under my roof does not portray me in a good light among our class. They deem it offensive and are outraged that I should act thus, and in my condition no less!

My own family have been neglectful in their correspondences' of late and sadly it is for the same reason. It seems charity is frowned upon in my society, unless it is a charity that has been deemed of acceptable character. I disagree. One can never decide what charity is worthy and what is not. I can neither send Margaret and her child back out into the cold, than I can abandon a helpless animal. I suppose that if I did have any feelings toward Captain John other than revulsion, I might reconsider, but I doubt it. It would be my duty to get to the bottom of her claims, and to determine if indeed the child was his and act accordingly. I might forgive his indiscretion eventually, but I cannot discard his child.

It is as I write the above line that it strikes me that I have behaved abominably towards his child that grows inside me. For the first time I truly stop and contemplate my actions towards something that is completely innocent, regardless of being Captain John's and I gently caress my belly. An innocent child. It is a thought I had weeks ago, but pushed it aside, too afraid to connect with it. I feel a shift deep inside me, and know it to be his child moving, my child. For now at this very moment, it is mine, not his, and I can give it love before he can destroy it.

And so our walk in the park brought out revelations of my own to reassure Margaret that she will have no need to return to the streets to sell her body, I will find a way to help her. In return she can work for me. Even as I speak the words I know the staff will not be happy with the arrangement, but Margaret is bored, she wants to work, and fill her days and feel useful; I understand that completely.

So here I sit after having a word with all of the staff together. I called for them all to come and hear what I have to say. If they wished to leave my employ then I'd feel no hard feelings, though I would miss them greatly. I now await their decisions with bated breath. I send Margaret out to buy some cloth for new dresses, as mine are becoming a little tight. In doing such, Annabelle springs to my mind and I fight off the sorrow that threatens to engulf me.

I sit quietly on the couch, enjoying the warmth emanating from the burning embers of the fire. Hargreaves will be in soon to check on it, but I hope not for a while. I can feel myself drifting into oblivion, a new connection made to my child and a new friend. I would never have contemplated such a thing, but there it is. Margaret is the closest thing I have to a friend and I would miss it terribly if I cannot find a way to hold onto her.

November 7th 1853

Morning is upon us and I arise with a sense of hope. After falling asleep by the fire I am woken hours later by Hargreaves who attempts to conjure the fire alive without waking me. Profusely apologising, he announces that he intends to stay, as do the rest of the household, so long as none of them have to 'wait' on Margaret. I agree and send my utmost thanks to them all for understanding, because I think they did.

Mrs Martins begged a meeting of which I happily obliged.

"Ma'am, we've all heard the screams, the cries, the shouts from the master, and the thud of fists against your skin. It made each and every one of us cringe and despise him for his cruelty. The brutality of Captain John is purely wicked and what he did to that poor girl … I blamed you for a time Ma'am, and I'm sorry for it." She began to cry and I beg her to sit and talk with me, but she refuses, and remains standing.

"We all know how the master can be. We understand Margaret's situation now. Will she be your companion Ma'am?" Margaret survived the only way she knew how. They may not like it, but they understand it.

As for me, I believe they know how lonely I truly am, perhaps more so than I knew myself, until recently. Having Margaret around has indeed helped me get through the weeks and it has gotten rid of my in-laws, and that alone is worth anything she might ask for!

"Yes Mrs Martins, Margaret will be my companion and help around the house wherever she is needed, if that suits you? And, thank you ..."

She left me then with a nod, a smile and a slight curtsey.

The day is spent in reading, and waiting for news. We walk in the park and I confess my new feelings towards this child. Margaret does not condemn me in any way, but smiles and links her arm through mine. John James lies asleep in the baby carriage that I'd bought for him.

November 9th 1853

*Margaret accepted my offer of staying,
and begins by starting on two new
dresses. She confesses to being minimal in
her sewing skills, but they outweigh mine,
and so I leave her to it. I feel remnants of
memories of the same actions with
Annabelle, who was indeed a marvel in
her designs and I wish I knew how she
fared. Perhaps I can ask Hargreaves if he
has had word of her? I sincerely hope
that she is living a happy life. I have to
decide how I will live mine. If nothing
else, Margaret has given me a new
strength, and I intend to act upon it.*

*I dress quickly, refusing the corset, which
Betsy is not happy about, but I wish to
breathe. I wolf down breakfast as my
appetite returns. I also find that I am
longing for eggs and insist on a second
helping of scrambled eggs, much to Mrs.
Martins' amusement.*

I send a telegram to my in-laws insisting they bring Captain John to his home. I am sick of waiting on them. Their lack of concern is both rude and dangerous for the baby. I receive an answer a mere hour later. They shall call on me for late afternoon tea and shall bring along their son.

No mention of 'my husband', only 'their son'. I can only guess at their meaning but strive to calm myself the rest of the day. I take another walk in the park along with Margaret, the babe and Betsy. It is a most pleasant few hours, sitting in the sun whilst Betsy and Margaret play with John James. It seems that Betsy is quite taken with the child, much to my amusement. I sit content on a bench, watching the ducks and swans glide over the pond, the midday sun warming my skin, though my hat keeps it off my face, I slip off my gloves. This is considered quite naughty in society, and it is rather cold, but I want to feel the air on my skin.

I have a late luncheon of cold meats, eggs and fruit, followed by a small nap, though I insist I will never fall asleep. Betsy wakes me after three o' clock with a cup of tea and biscuits from the cook. An hour later, they arrive.

I am waiting for them in the sitting room. The fire is lit and the room feels cosy. I do not get up and see the frown cross Gloria's face, and stifle a smile. My gaze follows the man that enters behind her, Captain John. He is looking around the room with curiosity, but eventually notices me and stops, holds out his hand and speaks, "My lady, it is a pleasure."

I cannot describe the shock that runs through me. This is my monster, my tormentor, the man I despise more than anything else. Yet here is a man who looks as I remember, and yet is different. There is no 'hardness' about him, only a faraway stare that makes him look faultless.

The man now standing before me is not the man who visited a prostitute, and gave her his son. This is not the man who viciously attacked a sixteen year old girl, and this is not the Captain John who made my life a misery for months. Most of his head is covered in white bandages and I find that I am curious to see beneath. I ask him to sit down.

I watch him staring around the room at various objects while Gloria and Sir George gaze at him, as if waiting for the light bulb to come on in his head, but I can see that nothing looks familiar to him, and that includes me. The Captain John who forced himself upon me time and time again, has indeed been killed in the war. The man sipping his tea is a younger version of him, held captive in his body.

We talk of everyday things like the park, the weather, the biscuits and cake, we barely touch as we wait to see if Captain John will remember anything; he doesn't. He'd bought this house only a few years before, but it seems his memory does not reach this far forward.

Sir George talks about the industry, and cricket which has Captain John joining in enthusiastically, and this astounds me. I have never heard him talk so openly with regards to his interests.

Gloria is talking about their horses, and how Captain John is hoping to go riding in due course, when Margaret bursts into the room. We discussed about introducing her to Captain John and his parents, and it had been agreed that on this occasion she would remain out of sight. It seems her eagerness to see him overwhelms her, and I can merely watch as she enters the room quickly, heading straight for my husband.

Sir George tries to bar her way, but she pushes past him and stands before Captain John who has risen as she entered. "John, do you know me? Please say you do, please ... Oh God, your head ...!"

Margaret's pleas are interjected by both Sir George and Gloria shouting at her to leave, and how dare she barge into the room. Forgetting of course that it is my room, not theirs. I remain silent, wanting to see how it plays out. By now Margaret has hold of Captain John, and is begging him to remember her and their son. At this point Sir George manhandles Margaret away from Captain John who is staring at the proceedings with such bewilderment, I actually feel for him. Sir George is pushing Margaret towards the open door where Hargreaves, who has heard the commotion, is loitering, unsure of what to do. Without thought, I push the nearest vase off the small table and let it fall to the floor with a loud crash. The sound puts an end to everyone's shouting, and they all turn to look at the source.

Gloria begins to make some remark about it being an expensive vase, but Captain John hushes her and walks towards me. The pieces have scattered, and the carpet is sodden from the water within; the flowers lay strewn upon the floor. I wait for the onslaught - none comes.

"Forgive me my lady. My parents are distraught and my behaviour is not pleasing."

I cannot find the words. This is not Captain John.

"Madam, I am truly sorry for my behaviour, I mean no offense."

I believe him and it unnerves me greatly.

"Captain ... John, I forgive you this offense. As for you three, sit down in my house quietly, and we shall conduct this affair calmly, am I quite clear?"

After calling for more tea during which time silence fell on the room, I am able to find a few moments to gather my thoughts on this man before me. I see the monster, yet he is a stranger to me, and to everyone else. Margaret is watching him closely from her chair closest to the door. Sir George is glaring at her and Gloria is staring into the fire. She looks exhausted and close to tears. The appearance of Margaret has pushed her nerves to the limit, I am sure of it. Captain John sits wringing his hands between his legs, looking like a lost and frightened puppy.

Once Hargreaves has left and tea is poured I give Margaret a slight nod and she leaves the room. Sir George begins to protest, but I refuse to listen and he gives up. Moments later Margaret re-enters carrying her son and sits down. The baby is asleep, thankfully, which helps us all remain civil and quietly spoken.

"John, may I introduce Margaret, a friend of mine and her son John James." Captain John immediately stands, and bows to Margaret, who shines at being seen by him. He remains standing, staring at her and the sleeping child for a while, before turning to his father. "Is it true? What I heard you say before about this woman and child?"

Sir George says nothing. I can see him desperately trying to find the right words, but in truth, it is easy. "Yes Captain, this is your son." I break the awkward silence and smile reassuringly. "It is easy to see the resemblance."

He slowly moves around the couch. He has a slight limp and I can see standing is painful, but he walks to where Margaret still sits. She watches his approach with such adoration I feel as if I am an intrusion in the room.

"We have no proof that this ... this... woman has borne your son John, it's a trick." Sir George finds his voice, but it falls on deaf ears, as Captain John bends down and examines his boy.

"He is remarkable Madam. May I hold him?"

Margaret relinquishes their son immediately. Gloria lets out a sob and holds a handkerchief to her mouth to stifle anymore noise. Sir George continues to glare at the woman who has, in his eyes, seduced his son to get money. I see differently. Margaret loves him and this child is born of that love.

Captain John finally gives his son back to Margaret and turns towards me with tears in his eyes. He fights to control his emotions as he returns to the couch. "My lady, if what I am told is true, then I have behaved in an un-gentlemanly manner towards you, my ... my wife. I cannot expect forgiveness after such an act of betrayal, but perhaps you can see it in your heart to help me remember our marriage, as it was? Sadly I have no recollections of you, nor of this lady, who has given me a son." He glances down then, and I think notices for the first time my own pregnancy, and puts his head in his hands.

Gloria immediately jumps up, "Come along, I think that's quite enough. He has terrible headaches and all of this has become too much."

"No Mother! I need to make amends to both of these women." He glances up at me, "Would you permit me to wander this house, perhaps something will trigger my memory ... I know it is an indulgence, especially after this revelation, but ..."

"No Captain, it is fine. Please feel free to roam; it is after all, your house."

It has been hours since Captain John left with his parents. Margaret retired to her room. I dine alone, and consume an enormous amount of food much to cook's delight and my astonishment. I then sit by the fire and reflect on the day's events.

Captain John wandered around the house for about an hour before his leg began to trouble him. Sir George and Gloria could contain their contempt no longer and stroll around the small garden, rather than remain in the room with Margaret. We barely speak; what is there to say? John James wakes and Margaret feeds him. It is as John James is lying on his back near the fire while Margaret gently plays with him that Captain John returned. He leans against the doorframe to ease the discomfort in his leg, but I can see that it pains him greatly. He takes in the scene before him. His mistress and their son, with his pregnant wife watching them. It is a concept too difficult for anybody to contemplate, and he abruptly takes his leave without informing us if he remembers anything during his wanderings.

November 10th 1853

I find myself considering the future. So far my child is growing healthily and I am into my fourth month. What will Captain John do? Will he accept his responsibilities to me, his wife and return home? Where would that leave Margaret? I do not wish her back on the streets, I gave my word and she has become a good friend which many find an impossible idea. A whore and a lady of good birth becoming good friends were unheard of.

I must admit, there is a large part of me who thrives on such a notion. I despise society and all of its rules. It is, after all, what got me into this awful situation, being married to a man I loathed, and I am nothing more than a pawn in the game of power and families. I envy the lower classes who can pick and choose who they wed, and say as much to Margaret, who laughs and tells me the 'lower classes' envy me my meals and warmth!

I am having difficulty sleeping, as my mind jumps from one idea to another. What if Captain John remains this agreeable man? How do I feel about being married to a stranger who behaves as a gentleman? What if the monster returns? Does he wish to remain married? Divorce is impossible, but we could have an annulment of sorts where we live apart perhaps, though neither can re-marry whilst the other is alive and he would have to pay me.

This remedy suits me the best I think, but I have no idea of his thoughts. To continue being his wife in all senses feels wrong, as if I am being wed off again to another complete stranger. I doubt any of my concerns matter to his or my own family, as long as we remain married and I produce a living and rightful heir.

And then of course there is Annabelle to consider. I find it repugnant to look upon the face of the monster who took away her childhood, in such a cruel way, and yet, I see no trace of such evil when this man looks at me. I am finding it difficult to see both men in the one body.

The Captain John I know so well, and this gentle, lost soul who feels such remorse at finding that he has fathered a child, whilst married, with a pregnant wife, no less. He has no notion of the pain and suffering he has caused. How can I even consider the possibility of continuing our marriage knowing that his body took a child's virtue without remorse?

November 11th 1853

Hargreaves came to me this morning after breakfast, though I barely touched a morsel. My nerves are stretched to their limitations, and so it is with regret that Hargreaves asks for a meeting. It seems the household is concerned for my well-being and for Margaret's child. The first I am flattered that I have conjured such devotion from my house. The second astonishes me so much I cannot answer for a long while on Hargreaves question, which is on everyone's lips – Is Captain John returning home?

I voice my surprise at the feelings towards Margaret's bastard, and remind him of how it had been so different only weeks earlier. He looks abashed, but stands his ground with dignity.

"How can we blame an innocent child for Captain John's behaviour? It would not be fitting. Besides, we have come to be fond of the child and his mother. Margaret is proving to be a kind-hearted woman who is earning everyone's respect, through her hard work and determination to leave her old ways behind her."

My attempts at keeping my face neutral fail. My continued silence becomes unbearable for the poor man, and he retreats. His leaving gives me a chance to contemplate the question that has kept me awake for most of the night. What to do about my husband? Of course, there is one thing nobody has considered so far, what does Captain John wish to do?

I saw the look on his face yesterday when he saw his son. If it had been a legitimate son, everything would be a lot easier, but he is not. The child in my belly is legitimate with no sure way of knowing if it is male.

I move around the room, unable to be at ease. My body is changing and I feel butterflies deep within me as the child moves. They are like fluttering of wings, a tickle beneath the skin and I feel the connection. I have completely stopped wearing tight corsets and admit to feeling free from their restraints. Today, I shall leave the house and walk. My coat shall hide me from any prying eyes, though I doubt anyone will notice. I care not a jot for gossiping tongues, and disapproving eyes. I am nineteen years old and feel double that age. I have endured so much in these last months; it has changed me, made me hard and I do not appreciate that. I miss my carefree days and think on them frequently. I believe my kindness has remained, but I see nothing of the girl I was anymore.

November 13th 1853

*My craving for eggs returns and I eat
two helpings of scrambled eggs, with
three rounds of toast. Betsy smiles at me
with a knowing grin, as does Margaret
who ventures into the room once I am
finished. We discussed her eating with me
as my friend, but we are aware that
although the household have accepted her
and the child, it is as one of their own,
and so she eats downstairs with Mrs
Martins and Betsy. It is acceptable that
she takes tea with me, and strolls as my
companion, but never my equal. This has
created a little jealousy with dear old
Betsy, and I must somehow remedy this,
along with all the other pressing issues.
I wake in the afternoon after falling
asleep on the couch beside the fire to the
ringing doorbell. Hargreaves informs me
that Gloria wishes to see me. I reluctantly
let her come in, and see the disapproving
look of my crumpled dress and perhaps a
few hairs out of place!*

It seems Captain John wishes to return to the house regularly in the hope of remembering something of his previous life. He has sent his mother to ask if this is agreeable to me in my present condition, as he does not want to endanger our child. I wonder who has really instigated such action, and who has truly spoken those words, as I very much doubt they have all been Captain John's concerns.

His parents may well have their son returned, but an heir was what truly mattered to them, or at least to his father. His brother may have two, but Captain John's child would be another member of the Harrison family and Sir George required both his son's to produce a multitude of offspring, so the name never dies out.

I'd heard that Sir George had been disappointed that Anne produced boy and girl twins as he'd hoped for two boys. Poor Anne, she was lost forever in that family. It has been made perfectly clear on many occasions, that what comes out of my body is all important; I am not.

"You look well." Gloria's attempt at kindness held an air of contempt and I refuse to be drawn in. She continues, "You're much further along this time. Four months? Are you eating, resting?"
"I am. I was resting when you called." Gloria looks uncomfortable for the first time. I see the strains of the last few weeks edged on her face, the black circles under her cold eyes, and the tightness around her mouth and shoulders. I let my guard down.
"The baby is doing well. I am eating and have a taste for eggs, pears and milk of all things. Did you have any strong desires whilst carrying John?"
I see the flash of shock at being asked such a personal question, and retreat back behind my wall. "Never mind, would you like some tea?"
We pass the next hour in an uncomfortable silence broken only by occasional pleasantries regarding my family, and I ask how Anne's pregnancy is progressing, only to be told she lost it weeks ago. They did not wish to tell me as they were concerned for my well being.

The anger I feel towards Gloria is immense. Why could she not have told me? Anne should not have to endure the pain of losing a child alone, but her family kept it a dirty secret.

Gloria finally departs with a message that Captain John is welcome the next afternoon. I have no notion if I am doing the 'right' thing, but in truth, I cannot stop my husband, the owner of this house, from returning and taking possession of everything within its walls. I own nothing, and that includes the child growing within my womb.

November 14ᵗʰ 1853

My night is long and arduous as I worry about today's event. Sometime in the early hours, I curl up with a pillow and cry myself to sleep. I am beginning to feel this child and I love it, want it, but I am so fearful of Captain John's behaviour, I worry of the child's life. If the monster returns, how can I allow this child to bear witness to such cruelty? Would he turn his evil intentions towards his own child? If it is a girl, what life will she have?

I fall into a troubled slumber and wake with a hunger so overwhelming I cannot stop my mouth from watering, as I make my way downstairs to the breakfast room. I devour the food with enthusiasm, much to cook's delight I'm told, and spend a pleasant hour in the garden. Though no flowers bloom, the scent of wet soil is pleasant, and the cold breeze, smells fresh.

Margaret pops her head out to check on me, as does Betsy, but both sense my need to be alone, and I am grateful for their kindness. Captain John is due in a couple of hours. The breakfast I enjoyed, now sits heavily in my stomach like a log, and I need the fresh air to aid in my recovery, along with short strolls among the flower beds, that come spring will be full of colour and perfume.

I need to be outside as the walls of my house feel as if they are closing in on me. The panic that I feel is so close to overwhelming me, that I have to be distracted, and the garden helps immensely. The fresh air also helps in keeping me awake. My sleepless night is catching up with me, and I can feel my eyes drooping.

November 15th 1853

Captain John arrived promptly yesterday, as though he had been loitering outside so as not to be late. The clock barely finished chiming the hour of two before he was knocking on his own front door; something I am finding extremely difficult. Hargreaves, who admits his master with a grim expression, and body language, that to any observer would know his contempt for this man.

Having almost drifted off to sleep in the garden, I make my way indoors and pace the house. Unable to sit still, I find myself in the hallway on his arrival, which surprises him greatly to find his 'wife' come to meet him. I believe it pleased him so much that I had not the heart to correct him, and he follows me into the drawing room. Hargreaves is close behind and waits while we seat ourselves comfortably, either side of the fire place. I order tea and Hargreaves leaves with a bow and a look of pure hatred towards Captain John, who, if he saw it, said nothing until Hargreaves left.

"It would seem I am not trusted among your staff my lady. It would appear that they do not wish you to be alone with me ... your husband."

"It is true sir, they are loyal to me." I did not know how to answer such a query. The man was a monster, yet a lamb sat before me.

Captain John shrugged. "I believe that I have a lot to answer for. My behaviour towards you, well, with this lady who now has my child, it is inconceivable to me that I allowed this to happen."

I glare at him. Seeing this pathetic man before me apologising for creating John James, yet nothing else, is unbearable. "You sir, have done more harm than creating a beautiful child. Can you not recall your behaviour towards me? You have defiled me sir on numerous occasions, and ruined a young girl's life with your monstrous behaviour. I find it contemptuous that you cannot remember such wicked deeds."

I was shaking badly and fought to control myself. The words were out in the open and I watched his face as they sank in.

"If I have committed such crimes, then let me be punished for them. You speak of acts of such horror, that I can barely believe that it was I who committed them and yet, seeing such behaviour from my own staff, I feel I must endure the truth of it. No staff would dare behave in such an impudent manner towards a guest or indeed, their master, and wish to save their employment."

I could feel my neck beginning to flush and took a long, shaky breath. "Indeed. They are loyal to me, and will come if called."

"I assure you Madam I shall give you no cause to call for aid." His voice was barely a whisper.

He was correct of course. Such behaviour would constitute a perfectly good reason to dismiss anyone who behaved in such a way to a guest of the house. I was making it clear that this would never happen, and Captain John understood perfectly. Tea arrived with Margaret, closely followed by Hargreaves who stood in the corner of the room awaiting his orders, but also making his presence known to our 'guest'. Captain John glances between them both, but says nothing. Margaret retreats once the tea is poured with a backward glance, and Captain John watches her leave with a strange expression.

"Do you remember her, John?" To use his name felt unfamiliar and awkward, but I persevere.

He does not answer directly, but stares at the door which is now closed. "I believe I do. It is not so much her face, it is more the 'essence' of her." As if saying such a thing to one's wife was inexcusable, he immediately apologises. "Madam, forgive me. It is inexcusable speaking of another woman in such a manner." He abruptly rubs his head and takes deep breaths. "Forgive me, I have pain that comes frequently, it will pass."

I sit silently and wait until he feels able to continue. Watching him in pain, makes me feel strange and I continue to watch in fascination. Eventually, he looks up at me and with a deep breath, I speak only honesty. "John, nothing in your behaviour has ever been gentlemanlike; Margaret and your son are the results of such. Living in this fog of memory is difficult on everyone, no doubt you worst of all. I cannot deny that seeing you is both terrifying and perplexing. I see the man who hurt me considerably in our marriage and yet, the man I see sitting before me is a stranger in my husband's shell. It is difficult to separate the two."

Captain John is silent for a long time and I let him be. I sip the hot liquid, enjoying the taste, and the steam, that rises from my cup. The biscuits look inviting, but my earlier hunger has long gone, as anxiety takes over. I make a mental note to nibble on a couple later, once John leaves.

"May I wander the house ... in your company, Madam?"

We spend an hour wandering the corridors and rooms of his home. We mostly keep silent, except for the odd question of a painting, or a piece of furniture or knick-knack. I am aware of the staff, as is Captain John. Though they keep out of sight, they make enough noise to let him know they are within reach. At the end of his tour, I expect him to leave, instead, having returned to the drawing room, he asks to see his son and Margaret, alone. "Would it be impertinent to ask for such a favour of my wife?"

"In these circumstances, I believe it is vital." I leave him then, and go in search of Margaret and John James myself. On hearing my request, she blooms, and it is all she can do not to run to where he is waiting. I admit to feeling a stab of jealousy at seeing this fondness. I wished for it myself. I wished for a love so deep, so passionate, it drove me wild with desire. What an odd thing, to see it in another woman, for my husband.

I consider Luke Babbleton and smile. Yes, I could feel that way for him. He held the key to my heart, but it would never be. If only we'd met sooner, how my life might have changed. He comes from a wealthy family. My father may have considered him a good match. I could be in love by now.

November 16th 1853

I had retired to bed, my diary written, when a soft knock at my door stirs me. Margaret stands, shaking and weeping, begging to be allowed in to speak with me. I admit her immediately and we curl up under the covers to keep warm. Although the fire is lit, its embers barely warm the room.

"You do not ask what passed between myself and John this day?" Margaret stares at me with such a longing, I am driven to reach out and clasp her cold hands.

"It did not seem appropriate Margaret. I know that if you deemed it important, you would tell me in your own time."

"He has asked if he might adopt our son, make him legitimate."

Her words took a moment to register their meaning and as I loosen my grip, she holds on tightly. "I would not allow it Madam, it would be wrong, and I told him as such. You carry his legitimate child, and I will not take that right away from you."

"I ... I am thankful for your concern, and grateful that you have a conscience in such a matter. I cannot believe he would not consider the child I carry in an important matter as this."

"No, he would adopt our son, and give him an education, a decent home and a family name to be proud of, but your child would always be his heir ... so long as it is male."

The fury I feel at such an outrageous action takes me by surprise. I shake with such venom that he could consider this. My child is just as important as Margaret's, regardless of its sex, and I say as much.

Margaret is tearful and regretting telling me, but I assure her it is for the best. I need to know what I am dealing with. Regardless of head injuries that take away memory, it did not take away attitudes towards women, being inferior to men.

Margaret pulls me close and holds onto me as I weep. I am not certain what I weep for, until it becomes clear in my mind as we talk. For Captain John to behave in such a manner, after I had welcomed a rapist, drunken wife beater into my home. It seems. Captain John's evil behaviour is coming through, he is leaking into this broken man and it seems his conscience is leaving him. The very thought of having to endure Captain John again is inconceivable to me and so I weep, for myself and the child whom he would happily abandon, depending on the sex, growing in my belly. I am frightened for my child and for myself.

November 21st 1853

Following Margaret's confession of what transpired between my husband and herself, I spend days in panic. Despite being reassured by Margaret that she will never allow it, we both know that as women, we have no rights.

Despite Captain John's injuries, he would still be entitled to take his bastard son, and make him legitimate if he so wishes. His only obstacle, that I can foresee, is his parents. Their attitude towards Margaret has never been hidden, and I doubt that their hostility will change. The child would never be welcomed by them, but they bore witness to Margaret's outburst about John James, and so they could be coerced into helping Captain John if my own child proves a disappointment. We wait with much anxiety for correspondence from any of them. Captain John has become quiet. Too quiet in my opinion. We spend the days walking, sewing, and I have written to my father.

November 24th 1853

My waiting has ended. We receive Captain John in the drawing room this morning. He looks pale and drawn and on enquiring, he informs me that sleep has been unforthcoming, as a migraine caused him days of pain.

I can think of nothing pleasant to say. I hold my breath and wait for him to speak. It takes him a moment to compose himself, and I use that time to compose my own mind and body. Looking at him causes me such anguish. I cannot commit to words what I would do to him if pushed.

My father was of little help, but assures me to hear what Captain John has to say first, before acting impulsively. He will aid me in my request at his earliest convenience if required.

"Margery, I have behaved abhorrently towards you, and it would seem that I have behaved thus since we first became married. I also believe that this union was forced upon you?" When I do not answer, he nods to himself and continues. "It would seem that my gross behaviour has been at times, violent towards you. I cannot express my remorse without sounding false, but I have no recollection of this person. I can only apologise for that man, and for not having the decency to remember such appalling monstrosities. I do you no justice by hiding it away somewhere in this broken brain of mine. That being said, I do you no justice being here at all. It would have been better if I'd died. At least then there would be some honour for me, and you could begin afresh, with our child."

He looked as though he was about to lean forward and reach out to me, but he hesitates. "I have no right to this child." He holds up his hand to stay my objections. "What I mean is, this child was born from violence on my part, and so I have no rights to it. I do not deserve such a gift. I made an error with your friend, Margaret, the other day. I have no doubts that she informed you of my offer." I nod silently and look away, unable to hold his stare.

"I did this out of shame, for I have wronged both of you and I deserve none of you. Oh I know what my parents say and have heard the tales of Margaret, and her past, and how we met, which only shames me more. I do not know what is to be done, but I must make amends to both of you. Jonathan James is my older son, but to adopt him as my own would cause our child to become secondary."

"My child will never be secondary, even if this is a girl I carry." My voice is thick with venom which surprises both of us. "Madam, I..."

"You will not adopt Jonathan James into this family, unless you place into a legal document that he will never inherit before this child I carry, regardless of whether this is a girl or boy. I understand that if this is a girl, it goes against everything society follows, like sheep, but I demand this one thing, for all that I have endured."

Captain John goes silent.

"If this is your course of action, I will abide by them and welcome Jonathan James as your son. I have become fond of both him and his mother, and have no objections to them living here with me, however, if you go against this Captain John, hear this, I will expose you as the monster that you are, and will shame your family name, till nobody in good society will receive you, or your parents."

Captain John bows his head and I can see him biting his upper lip. It is a risk to voice my thoughts out loud to him, but one I can no longer endure in silence. I have to know, for my own child's sake, if he is still a monster, or a man fighting to regain his honour, as he says he truly wishes.

"I agree with you Margery, wholeheartedly, and it shall be done at once."

I lean forward and study him carefully. "You would do this for our child?"

Captain John reaches out and takes my unresisting hand. "I would indeed Madam, to gain your trust and look honourably in your eyes. If it will help to heal the wounds that I have caused, then it shall be done."

November 30th 1853

Today I am asked to call into the offices
of Captain John's solicitors, whereupon I
read and sign the document that pledges
that the child I carry this day, will be the
sole beneficiary of Captain John's
inheritance unless I miscarry again,
whereupon, it would move to John James.
In the possibility of another child, then all
wealth would be shared equally between
both children.
I read the last line of the document with
a bitter taste in my mouth. I catch
Captain John watching me closely.
'Possible children.' If I decide to allow him
to continue as my husband, and we have
more children. As if I have any choice in
the matter? He can return to his home at
any time. According to Gloria, his
recuperation is going well and the wound
is healing. His headaches give him much
pain, but they are lessening. I fear which
man will arise from his injuries, once
they heal – the monster, or the
gentleman?

On my return home, I inform Margaret of the outcome, and she seems content. Her child will not starve on the street, or rot in some workhouse, but will be brought up in a respectable home and can be my child's companion. Captain John is his guardian, and Margaret is my friend and companion, to the outside world. The tongues will wag and the gossip shall indeed be scandalous, but for our children, we can endure.

December 5rd 1853

Christmas is fast approaching; my first as a married woman, though Captain John remains with his parents. It suits us all. Our household has a good routine and I leave them to do their jobs. I worry about Hargreaves. I believe that he is struggling with this man before him, knowing he ruined his niece, yet to speak of it, may jeopardise his position. Also, Captain John has no recollection of us, so to accuse a man of a crime, he cannot remember, seems unjust.

Surely justice cannot be served on a man incapable of memory to that crime? It is unfair to the victim, and it breaks my heart, but there must be another way of gaining justice for the crimes committed against us, that gives Annabelle and myself peace of mind.

I call Hargreaves into the study today and ask after Annabelle. I am informed that the business is doing well, and there is talk of opening another, if this one continues as successful as it has been.

"Does Annabelle know of Captain John's return and what state?"

Hargreaves shrugs. "I see no point in mentioning that man to my niece, Madam. She is living up in Scotland now, let her be."

I agree and he takes his leave. I am not in the least surprised that Annabelle is doing so well, and I am happy for it. I look at her dresses she made me with regret, but I cannot wear them now as my figure is much too big.

I feel the child moving fairly frequently. Gloria insists that Doctor Hobson see me and he gives me good health. Gloria has since sent me a bouquet of flowers and invitations to parties where I might sit comfortably. I stare at the flowers, and the Christmas invites, and am not sure how to feel on receiving them. It is as if I have passed a test to reach five months pregnant.

December 12th 1853

I sent caution to the winds these last days. I have been received at two parties of Bridge, and enjoyed a dinner party at this house tonight, with Captain John and both parents. We deem it wise to keep Margaret away, for now. Let the parents get used to the idea. It is a pleasant evening on all three accounts. I have forgotten how lovely it can be to be out, with people of all ages, and just talk, catching up on gossip and being seen.

I must admit, I feel wonderful now. My sickness is gone, I have a rosy complexion, and I feel what can only be described as happiness. I believe it is the baby promoting such feelings. I feel such a connection with it. I yearn to feel it move every day. Occasionally I poke my stomach, just to get a response. Captain John is also most attentive. I am finding his company to be fairly amiable, if I can ignore the deep rooted fear and revulsion that returns abruptly. I find myself flinching away from his presence, and making excuses to remove myself. He does not enquire of it or pursue me when I move away; I believe he finally has a conscience.

December 24th 1853

Captain John spends most of today with Margaret and me. His father comes for lunch and informs us of the ongoing war. I watch Captain John's face as his father tells us of the reports that British troops have very little to do besides the occasional battle. It was one of these small skirmishes that wounded John, and I see how much it bothers him.

He has no recollection of his men, his regiment or his friend, Lord George Paget, who has already sent word of his worries regarding Captain John and will return immediately once the war is over. How odd that only months before I wished my husband far away, and dead. I watch the shadow of the man before me, sorting garlands for the tree. My hatred of him has not diminished, and yet, I find that I can look beyond that, and see a man I might endure, if necessary. I have the upper hand now, and it feels liberating.

The rest of the day is spent decking the tree Hargreaves brought home and decorating the room. We can smell the preparations for our evening dinner. We have eight people coming – parents and old friends. Tonight, Margaret will be joining us as my guest.

Both parents have been informed, and both are content enough to come. I believe it is purely curiosity on my parent's part, but they have been warned to behave, and everyone obliges. A fine night is had by all. My father spends rather a lot of time talking to Margaret, much to my amusement, but besides a few ill-disguised looks from Gloria and my mother, the evening is a success.

December 26th 1853

Yesterday was a pleasant day. Gifts were given and everyone was smiling, the day was light and agreeable. We ate Christmas dinner after mass and played games of all kinds and made merry. Captain John joined Margaret and me for the most part, but begged to leave us as darkness fell, due to his commitments to his parents who expected him for dinner. Margaret watched him leave with such a sorrowful look on her face, I felt compelled to embrace her for comfort.

Today we are spending the day indoors as snow begins to fall by midday. Margaret and I play cards and spend a most pleasant afternoon. By the evening, I feel so tired, we have a light supper and I retire to bed to rest. And now, here I sit, the fire is blazing in my room and I am content. I never considered myself to feel such a feeling in this marriage, but I cannot lie, I am, at this moment, content.

December 31st 1853

The last day of this most horrid of my years. I married, I turned nineteen and I lost a child, but carry another. My husband, a monster who went to war and came back injured and a stranger. He continues to suffer his headaches and his leg aches from time to time. He has sent his apologies for not visiting since Christmas day.

Tonight, I am invited to join Gloria and Sir George, my parents, Katherine, David and friends in bringing in the New Year at their home, and so preparations need to be made as I will be expected to stay over and not return at such a late hour. Margaret, regrettably, though not surprisingly, has not been invited, but assures me that she is agreeable to this lack of kindness and will enjoy her evening, with my household staff. In truth, I must admit to wishing to stay at home, as the merry making sounds so much more fun.

My journey to his parents' home, takes a little longer due to snow and ice, but I finally arrive early afternoon and am immediately given tea, and a light luncheon in my room, and told to rest. I did indeed sleep for a while and feel much better for it.

By the time Betsy has helped me into a dress and done my hair, she tells me guests are already arriving and my stomach growls loudly through lack of sustenance. Betsy, looking a little grumpy for not being allowed to stay at home, saves me from embarrassment, and produces a small plate of home-made biscuits and blackberry cordial from Gloria's cook, who apparently likes me! We help ourselves hungrily, and I am ready to go downstairs.

As I walk down the stairs, Captain John is waiting for me and offers me his arm. I can see no reason to object, and take it. We stride into his parent's library, as husband and wife.

January 3rd 1854

I am home. I remained at Captain John's parent's home until yesterday, as the snow continued to make travel difficult. It was decided that in my condition, it would be prudent to remain safely indoors.

For once, I did not argue. Their attitude towards me is fairly agreeable, as if I have behaved well enough to deserve their time and forgiveness. Though I ask for none of it, I find the atmosphere easier to tolerate.

Both Richard and Anne were also staying, along with their children who thankfully, stayed outdoors for the most part, building various snowmen and women and throwing snow balls at anything that moved. My attempts at conversation with Anne were met with limited responses and downward glances. This woman is older than me and yet, she reminds me of a mouse, cowering beneath a giant, hissing cat. I look at Richard and I see a prowling animal, just waiting to catch his prey.

I truly feared him once, but now I am to be a mother, something within me has shifted. I may have been a victim of abuse, but not anymore - and he knows it.

I catch him looking at me, but as before, he would continue to leer. Now, he looks away quickly, and I smile to myself. He truly is pitiable. No lover of women, but a boy who needs to dominate to feel powerful. How sad that both brothers have been educated in such a manner.

January 7th 1854

It is good to be home. Even though I was treated adequately, the comfort of being at home can never be replaced, especially when surrounded by the people I care for. I do not have to consider etiquette when I wish to leave a room or fill my growing belly. My yearning for eggs became so overwhelming whilst at my in-laws home, I felt obliged to send Betsy to the cook to supply me with enough to satisfy this body. Somehow it got back to Gloria, and before long, the whole household knew of my hunger. I was most embarrassed.

Captain John continued to be most attentive during my stay and we saw in the New Year together. He begged my indulgence and kissed my hand. The feel of his moustache made me recoil as I felt it on my skin, but I did not remove my hand from his grasp. I believe he felt my shudder and with a slight bow, he released my hand.

He has visited us twice since, and I am encouraging him to spend more time with his son and Margaret, whilst I rest, or read in my room. I see his dilemma and reassure him that I am content with the arrangement.

It is a strange relationship to be sure. The three of us, bound together now by children and honour. How different it might have been for Margaret, if Captain John had not been injured. Would he have accepted the child publicly? And what of me? I have no doubt his behaviour towards me would indeed be abominable and I wonder if I would have found the courage to keep my new friend.

How strange it is for me to have such a dear friend, as I have come to cherish Margaret. We confide and debate, we sew together, and create all sorts of things from dresses to cushions, though, sadly, mine are lacking.

I confess all of my fears to Margaret, and she tells me her own. Today Margaret confides her fear at having to return to her previous occupation. She begins to tell me of her first encounter with a stranger and I beg her to stop. I can only promise that she will never have to return to that life, so long as I live, and Captain John keeps his word. She thanks me most ardently, and we cry together over our open wounds.

January 9th 1854

Captain John visits this morning. After his departure, I am left speechless, and thoughtful, on his request - he wishes to move back into his own home.

He spoke gently and sincerely I believe, on my own welfare and that of our unborn child and wishes me no ill. He assures me that he will not resume his husbandly duties in the bedroom until such a time that it happens naturally, but he feels the need to return and does not wish to burden his parents longer than necessary.

"I hope to move back into my home." His anticipation is plain to see and I have to look away. "Have you not considered it Madam? Despite my previous behaviour towards you, we do have a child and so surely it is wise for us to live as a family ... Margery?"

How can I respond? It is after all his house, not mine, and I say as much. I do not believe that I manage to convey any enthusiasm for his returning, but I accept its inevitability and inform the staff and Margaret. She takes the news well, before remembering my feelings on the matter and shows some constraint.

The staff do not bother to hide their revulsion at his return and some voice a possibility of leaving to find work elsewhere. This causes me the most stress and I beg them to remain on a trial period, for my sake.

I despise the idea of sharing anything with another man who could control me. I have grown used to my freedom as a war widow, despite my husband still being alive. In the eyes of the law, I am still his property, even if he doesn't remember me.

I wish I could speak with my mother or Katherine, but they are so entrenched in the system as doting wives, they will never understand my hatred of being someone's possession. I do not believe that my mother loved our father upon their marriage, but she found something akin to love and respect by the time we were born. Katherine adored David on meeting. I can be quiet no longer.

When I look at him I see only pain and suffering. I see the humiliation and the horror of what he has inflicted on me without regard for my well being. I see his face twisted in contempt as he raises his fists, and I see the pleasure it gives him to use my body despite my objections. I see his hatred of women and the need to own us. I see the pitiful, broken body of a young girl whom he has ravished against her will without pity and now, he does not even remember his actions. All of this I tell him.

He sits, white-faced and eyes down, as I inform him of every terrible thing he has done since our marriage. It is all I can do to keep my voice from rising with each monstrous action I recall for him to hear. As I speak of Annabelle, my voice does break with emotion, but I persevere, until at last, I sit back exhausted. My throat parched, I ring for tea, but more importantly, I need to be reassured of other people within the household. When Hargreaves appears almost immediately, I manage a weak smile in gratitude; he has been outside the door, my safety, his only concern, as promised.

Captain John did not stay for tea but with a polite apology, he leaves me, asking that I consider his request. It is this that leaves me speechless. After all the horror I convey, he still wishes to return. Does this show a concern for my wellbeing? I think not.

January 13th 1854

It has been four days since I last heard from my husband or his family. This morning I receive a short letter informing me that Gloria and Sir George will be away in the country until spring overseeing some alterations to their country estate. They will be obliged if I can inform them of the birth of their grandchild immediately, and they will make the journey to receive it. I tear up the telegram and throw it in the fire. They have left to allow Captain John time alone to ponder his future. This child is due in May, they will be back in town before then. They will only be obliged to show any gratitude on their grandchild if it is a boy; they care not a jot if it is a girl.

As if answering me, I feel a large kick to my back and groan with the discomfort. Hargreaves, who is always hovering near-by, comes to my aid immediately, and helps me to the drawing room and builds up the fire as the January winds blow outside. He also fetches a rug to wrap around my legs. I do not have the heart to tell him I need to walk about the room, but wait until he has left to fetch Margaret, and thus begins my turn of the room.

I catch my breath a few times as each sharp kick catches me under the ribs, or a fist touches a nerve. I find that if I walk slowly, the babes movements grow less, as if my walking somehow eases the child into sleeping. By the time Margaret appears flustered and concerned, I am well enough to put her and Hargreaves at ease and ask for tea and some of cook's homemade scones.

Both looking openly reassured, they leave me to fulfil the task required. My appetite, despite the stress of Captain John, has returned enormously, and I find myself desiring all sorts of sweet things at unthinkable times of the day! I have been reared to accept the times of breakfast, luncheon and dinner and the times for tea in-between, but convention be damned, my child wants it, and so, he or she gets it. My craving for eggs has gone, but pears and milk continue.

Margaret joins me whilst I wolf down three scones with jam and cream, a pear and two cups of tea. I sit back sated and drowsy afterwards and listen as Margaret reads from a book of poems. We have taken to finding these quiet moments when Jonathan James is taking a nap, and I believe we both find them most pleasant. I have encouraged Margaret to continue her education, and know that she has read through many books in the library in her haste to prove her worth.

I am not sure how long they let me sleep, but I wake to Margaret's gentle but insistent shaking and stare up at her tear-stained face. Both Hargreaves and Mrs Martins are also in the room. Cook is holding the baby who is wiggling in her arms.

"Oh Madam, Margery, you must wake."
I blink my eyes to clear them and stare at each in turn before returning my gaze to Margaret, who now stands before me, wringing her hands in despair, as tears wash down her face.

"What is going on? What has happened?"
I fight to clear my head having been woken from a deep sleep.

"Oh Margery, it is the end of me."
I glance at Hargreaves for some confirmation, but it is Mrs Martins who answers.

"We received two telegrams Madam, not five minutes ago. From Captain John. One is for you, the other ..."
I glance back at Margaret who is now clutching the said telegram to her bosom, then back at Hargreaves who holds out the other; I do not take it. I do not need to. Captain John is dead.

I feel only a stabbing fear that my child's future will be in jeopardy somehow and make a quick mental note to check the document that bears all our signatures. Damn the coward! I look across at Margaret whose sobs have escalated, and she is being helped to the opposite armchair by Hargreaves who has a look on his face that I can't read. Pity perhaps? Our eyes meet and he quickly bows his head. No, pity for Margaret maybe, but he holds nothing but contempt for the man he has to call master, and I for one do not blame him. I hold out my hand for the telegram and read it.

'Madam, Margery, my wife, I have done as promised, regardless of the sex of our child, it shall be highly cared for as my heir. I am assured that all is signed and sealed and is lawful. I cannot regret what I cannot remember. It would have been better had I died a gentleman in war, but I believe that God kept me alive to make amends. Do not think too harshly of me. Your husband. Captain John Harrison.'

I let the paper fall and reach out for Margaret's telegram; I have a right to know.

'Margaret, though I cannot remember our time together, I am honoured to know I have a son. John James will be cared for, have no fear on that score. I am sorry; it cannot be any other way for me. Do not think ill of me in this cowardice action. I am making amends for my crimes. Live for us both. Captain John Harrison.

Damn the man! He knew he should have died in battle. There is no honour here and Captain John knew it. There was only the mess a stranger had left behind and he did not have the courage to pick up the threads of his old life, regardless of whether he remembered or not.

I feel such an array of emotion it is difficult to choose which one I wish to feel. Anger and pure hatred towards him for all I was made to endure, yet, I feel my resolve to loath the monster waning. How could I despise a man who didn't remember his crimes, and showed a compassionate side by making sure his family were cared for? I saw a different man these last few months. One I could tolerate, perhaps in time, comes to respect, but there would always have been the internal fear that the monster might return. I even contemplated allowing Margaret to resume any 'wifely' duties with my blessing. My emotions truly are a mess.

January 16th 1854

I have neither the heart nor the inclination to write for a few days. Our time has been spent in mourning, though in truth, I have done very little. The tears I shed have been for my child and our future. I feel only anger towards my husband. My only conciliation is that as his wife, I am secure. The document is legally binding and all is well on that score.

His parents returned late last night. They sent a message to inform me of their homecoming and will call on me at their earliest convenience. My own parents are due today. Captain John's suicide has sent shockwaves through our community, and from what I understand I am to feel shame for his cowardice. Apparently, Gloria is inconsolable. Sir George is in shock and was heard to cry out, "John, what have you done? A coward is my son ... A coward!" I know nothing of Richard's behaviour. Of my own, I keep a silent, outward appearance as I wear my widow's outfit and hide my face with a thick, black veil. It is for the best. I cannot grieve for the man.

Margaret moves around the house in quiet shock. She does her chores and cares for John James, but she has lost her passion for life. I attempt to comfort her, but she flees the room in tears; I do not follow her. Mrs Martins and Hargreaves have both spoken with me of their own thoughts on the matter and I understand their feelings completely, as they mirror my own.

The funeral is tomorrow. Despite the taking of his own life, he is being interred in the family vault as the family wish it. The vicar does not protest as loudly as expected, but why would he? Sir George pays a large contribution to the church's upkeep. If he wants his son to be buried within its holy ground, then it shall be so. The coffin is kept closed throughout the vigil due to the severe wound to his head. It was deemed best for me that I did not witness the horror of it.

January 17th 1854

*Today is my husband's funeral. I find
that as we stand around the vault, I do
indeed feel something akin to sorrow;
that takes me by surprise. Tears do fall
down my cheeks and my parents give me
comfort. Since their arrival yesterday,
Mother and Father have shown me
nothing but concern and kindness. It
seems to have one's husband commit such
an act brings out love for their daughter.
I later find out their 'concern' is aimed at
the wellbeing of our child, and its
inheritance. Once they are assured on the
matter, they seem at ease.*

*On our return to the house, Gloria is
taken upstairs to the guest bedroom, as
she fainted at the churchyard. She did
indeed look pale and sickly and I feel
concern for her and assure Sir George
that they must remain until she is able to
travel.*

Of Margaret, there is no sign. It was inconceivable that she be allowed to come to the funeral, however, I instruct her to visit his grave once we have departed. She readily agreed. Now, hours later, Margaret has still not returned with John James. I send word to Mrs Martins to ask, but no-one has seen her since this morning.

Dinner is a morose affair. Hardly anyone touches cook's fine meal, me included. I ask Betsy to make me something later and bring it up to my room on a tray. I have an enormous appetite, but it feels heartless to enjoy food, whilst the group mourns a man.

January 23rd 1854

Captain John's solicitor came this morning. He wished to speak with me in private, which was easy, as Gloria and Sir George departed for home yesterday and my own parents have gone into town. I saw him in the library and must admit to feeling apprehensive about this visit.

Captain John's instructions were clear. I would be awarded so much per year, and what I did with it was up to my own conscience. Knowing I would support Margaret and his son, he'd given me the wealth to do it, and our child would be granted the rest. A small fortune had been put in place until he or she reaches eighteen. However, there was still enough to allow me to live in relative comfort. There was also a small trust, kept by Sir George that would become my child's once they reached adulthood. Captain John had instructed his solicitor to inform me of everything so that I did not worry over such things.

I stare at the ageing man for a long time, trying to understand his information. I abruptly put my handkerchief to my face, to suppress a smile. The poor man thinks I am distraught and orders a glass of water from a hovering Hargreaves, believing that I will fall down in hysterics or the vapours at any moment.

I allow him to console me, merely to help my cause if there should ever be any falsehood accusations. I believe I gave a fair performance of shock. I eventually reassure the solicitor that I am well, and he leaves, somewhat gratefully. Once he is gone, I allow myself to smile fully. I gently touch my bulging bump and tenderly stroke it whilst I contemplate life without Captain John.

January 26th 1854

Since the death of John, I have had a steady stream of visitor's cards, left for me at the door. I keep myself to myself and this behaviour has been misconstrued as grief - let them think it, I care not a fig. Margaret finally reappeared the day after his funeral, but barely speaks. She remains for the most part, in her rooms with her son; no one has interfered with her grief on my orders. She has the right to mourn the man she loved, even if society deems it immoral. I will not deny

my friend her grief. Perhaps it is right
that one of his women feels something of
his death.

January 28th 1854

I have been sitting for so long this
afternoon following a lovely luncheon
with my in-laws and parents who visit,
my back is beginning to ache and I stand,
a little unsteadily and cry out in pain as
a foot kicks out on my spine. Believing I
am in labour, Hargreaves hurries in and
sends for Dr Hobson. Margaret comes
rushing downstairs and by then, I am
reassuring all concerned that it is just a
kick. I assure them all is well and merely
need to stretch my legs and back.
Gloria gives me such a venomous look,
that I dare to complain for nothing more
than a little backache. I glare back, which
only brings on more of her uncontrollable
tears and wailing that I am heartless.

My mother sits, unsure what to do, and her indecision is her downfall. I note the look of disappointment on her face as I am escorted out of the room, heading for my bedroom in need of relief.
I thought the day would never end.

February 2nd 1854

My parents remain, though for most of it, I have spent in my own rooms. My father leaves after lunch today to visit the town; my mother comes in search of me. She finds me sitting in my window seat, holding one of my books, though I have not read a page of it. The wind howls outside and hail has just finished hammering against the glass. I am staring down at the small white balls of ice when she enters. I hear the knock and door opening, but I was expecting Betsy. My mother surprises me, and she sees it. She has the decency to look ashamed.
"I'm the last person you wish to see Margery?" she asks in as light-hearted manner as she can muster.

"I merely did not expect you Mother. I thought that you would go into town with Father." I refuse to make room on the window seat and so she sits on the end of my bed.

"Would that have been preferable to you?"

I do not know how to answer and she sees me hesitate and looks sad. "The severe weather changed my plans and so I wish to spend time with my daughter."

I wait.

"I am sorry, Margery." I barely hear the words. She hangs her head and so the words are muffled.

"You are apologising?" She has my attention now.

"I should have acted on your information regarding your problems, and I did not, believing that it would sort itself out. In truth, I have no notion what must be done in such situations. You are ... were his wife and so he had rights to do whatever he saw fit."

"Whatever he saw fit? And what of my rights? What of yours as a parent? I cannot conceive the notion that I would allow this child to marry without love. I have endured such horror Mother, and for what? For two old friends to make an alliance of some kind? Was my life part of a deal that I have not been made aware of perhaps? I wish you could help me understand."

Mother merely shakes her head and wipes her eyes. I move off the window seat, too angry to be still. I get no further than three steps when a pain shoots through me and I gasp, clutching the wall for support.

What happens in the next hours is a little blurred, for I have very little recollection. Labour came on abrupt and painfully. My waters broke within minutes of my standing and Mother took charge. I recall Betsy running into the room quickly followed by Margaret, who has a few brief, curt words with my mother until another shout from me silences them both into accepting a truce, and helping me onto the bed.

The doctor is called and the day turns into early evening when Heather Louise Harrison is born to me. She lives a few brief moments, before dying in my arms. She is small and perfect. Her eyes are closed, but I imagine her eyes to be blue. She has fine hair on her head.

I know that I am dying. The bleeding cannot be stopped and although I feel weak, and have perhaps only moments left, I have asked Doctor Hobson to give me time alone with my child. He arrived too late and I see the grief of it written on his face. He cannot save me, as he could not save my daughter, but I wish him no ill will.

I believe Heather was destined to die. I have felt these terrible aches in my back for days, but did not realise their meaning. Margaret is distraught, but I assure her that it is not her fault and her son is cared for and thank her for the friendship we enjoyed. My mother begs me to live, but she knows it cannot be. I forgive her and Father and wish them joy; we will hold each other again.

I instructed her where to find my diary and begged her to allow me this time to leave my last entry. I would wish many changes in my life, but here it is. Would a change have altered my life so as not to have Heather? I would not wish it so. Heather, my darling daughter, saved me. She showed me that I can feel love, even from such dreadfulness. I will wish this love on the world ... I found the joy of it, if only briefly. Love is stronger than hate. For those reading these pages, believe it is so and live, for me. We will not be parted long and I give thanks for it.

Your friend,

Margery Rose Harrison (Blake)

Notes from the Author

This is completely fictional, yet I wanted to portray the reality of a woman's life in 19th century England. A woman lost all rights once married. Before the passing of the 1882 Married Property Act, everything the woman owned became the property of the husband's once married, even her wages became his if she worked. The women were expected to be dependent on their husbands, especially the upper classes. Once married, it was almost unheard of for a woman to obtain a divorce on any grounds. The Matrimonial Causes Act of 1857 did give men the right to divorce their wives on the grounds of adultery. Women could not get the same rights even if the husband had been unfaithful. The children were considered the man's property, even after divorce and wives could be prevented from seeing their children.

Dedication

I dedicate this book to all the strong women who have helped and supported me through this life so far. You know who you are, ladies.

About the Author

P.J Roscoe is the author of three books so far. When not writing, she holds various healing workshops. Paula is a qualified counsellor, holistic therapist and healing movement and drumming facilitator, and trained volunteers to become Cruse Bereavement Care support workers for six years. She lives in North Wales with her husband of twenty-two years, their daughter and a multitude of animals.

www.pjroscoe.co.uk
Twitter@derwenna1
Facebook -
https://www.facebook.com/storyladyauth
or/
www.crimsoncloakpublishing.com

Books by the author
Echoes
Freya's Child
Adventures of Faerie Folk – Volume 1
*

Books coming soon
Between Worlds (December 2016)
Where Rivers Meet (2017)
Adventures of Faerie Folk – Volume 2
(2017)
Various short stories in anthologies
Steps in Time (Time goes by …)
Love Alters (Inevitable Love)
Travels in Time (A Mother's Love)
(Crimson Cloak publishing)

Acknowledgements

I would like to thank Sue Miller - from <u>All Words Matter</u> for helping with the editing and marketing of this new venture and Cal who created the book cover.